SMOKE & MIRRORS

FIRE COMPANY NO. 143

DANIELLE BROOKS

DEDICATION

This book is dedicated to all the single mamas! As a single mom, I know how difficult it can be to balance life as a mom and as a woman. Let this book serve as a reminder that you deserve love, too!

I would also like to send a special thank you to Shantel and Tomorrow. Thank you for being a part of the process, commenting, laughing, and truly enjoying the journey of Tevin & Joni as I wrote. Your support is forever appreciated. This is also dedicated to you!

Happy Reading!

Mama gotta have a life, too.

    -Jody's Mama, *Baby Boy*

A NOTE FROM THE AUTHOR

Hey, just a quick heads-up—this book may touch on some emotionally heavy topics, including past trauma and complicated relationships, and a few things in between. While I've written it with care, some parts might hit close to home. Please take care of yourself as you read.

ONE MORE NOTE

If you love this book, please be sure to rate, review and share on your favorite platforms, especially Amazon, Goodreads, and Storygraph. Your ratings and reviews are what help readers find your favorite indie authors. Even if it's just a few words or a star-rating, it's appreciated!

Now, really, go ahead and enjoy the book :)

PROLOGUE

―

JONI

―

"Ladies and gentlemen, I now present to you for the first time Mr. and Mrs. Benjamin and Fallon Deacon!"

"Alright, now!" I gush, as Deacon dips Fallon and smooches her against the picture-perfect backdrop of Lovey's Cliff —sunny skies and Lovey's Bay rushing below. Fallon's little muscular thigh climbs up Deacon's hip, and the way he mashes his fingers into her exposed thigh tells me all I need to know—he has her for breakfast, lunch, *and* dinner. I know this because I've seen it with my own eyes over the last year. I really like him for her, though. He treats my girl well.

"Be careful, you two!" Nina calls out. She rubs her round belly, a cautionary tale only she can deliver. Denzel closes the space between them, placing his hand atop hers before he pecks her cheek, sending the newly-weds off with a proud grin.

I beg Nina's difference, retorting, "No, *don't* be careful! We need you back *nice and pregnant*!"

"Oh, my God!" Fallon squeals in response, throwing her hand at me as she recovers from her smooch. She comes up with the help of Deacon to balance her as they pose for the flicker of cameras. My playful remark brought laughter to the few people who were witnesses to the nuptials at Lovey's cliff.

All my girls are living in their happily ever afters now. Fallon and Deacon just spontaneously wed and are now heading off to the islands for her brother's wedding. Meanwhile, Nina is planning a fall wedding while preparing for the birth of her baby. A lot of love is filling the salted air in Lovey's Bay, and I can't help but think about my drab of a love life. At some point, I want to plan a wedding and get my waist snatched to the Gods in a flowing dress and walk down somebody's aisle to my tall, dark, and handsome…

"Tevin, you're next!" Deacon hollers as he revs up the engine of the old school ride he and Fallon now occupy. He points at Tevin, who stands behind me, and winks.

"Shiiiiit!" Tevin drawls, laughing. "I ain't drinking none of that water y'all are drunk on!"

Deacon shakes his head before giving the engine one last rev and peels off down the two-lane highway.

"Why you gotta be so crass?" I ask, turning my nose up at him as I look up and over my shoulder at him. It's more of a playful question than anything. His blunt, no-filter demeanor is part of what draws me to him.

He shrugs, taking no accountability. "I didn't do nothin'." He inches closer, as if there was any space left between us, and leans in, murmuring, "You ain't giving me no play, just booty."

I fight to remain unbothered by his words. My mouth twitches as I fight back a smirk, hiding the sting of his words well enough that he doesn't notice. I narrow my eyes at him and let a half smirk settle, counter, "You weren't complaining last night."

A stifled laugh rumbles in his throat as his eyes grow dark and daring. His words come out with a slight edge. "Nope, I wasn't. Still not. Just stating facts, Lil' Bit."

"Whatever." I am uncertain of what is simmering between us, whether it's sexual tension or some other tension, but I want neutral grounds. I roll my eyes and twist my mouth into a smirk.

Tevin. He's an itch I just can't stop scratching. He's fine, with honey brown skin and facial hair always neatly trimmed due to his career as a firefighter, showing off his boyish yet striking features. He towers over me at six feet three, over my five-five frame, sporting a slim build like a basketball player—you know, skinny but with nice muscle tone. He's different than what I've dated in the past in features, but that's probably what attracted me to him. That, and also the rumor that the tall, slim ones were always packing—if you know what I mean.

The rumor? All facts. Tevin is packing a monster and his sex drive—more like kicked into overdrive and never stalling. This could probably be explained by his high-adrenaline career and our five-year age difference, but who really cares? Am I complaining? Hell, no!

Young, fine, and an Energizer Bunny? Your girl is in heaven!

Aside from the Big 3, Tevin's fun and uncomplicated, which is why I take most of what he says with a grain of salt. He is so unserious.

That boy ain't trying to marry me, I reflect, recalling his statement. For some reason, my inner dialogue makes my heart sink with an unwarranted disappointment. I sip in a sharp breath, a jolt to my system I need to remember, I'm not supposed to care.

"Ready to head out?" I ask, noticing the crowd thinning out. Mr. and Mrs. Deacon, Nina and Denzel, and the Reverend were either entering their cars or pulling away, leaving Tevin and me standing in the middle of the sandy outlook.

He gives me a shrug again. "Yeah, if you are. Whatchu doing later?"

I look down at my watch for no particular reason. I had nothing going on that required me to care about the time. "Nothin'. No plans."

Tevin tilts his head towards the barbecue spot across the way. "Wanna get some Baby Dee's and chill on the beach for a bit?"

"Do you see what I have on?" I ask, glancing down at the white, flowy summer dress and strappy heels I wear.

Tevin raises an eyebrow, quizzing, "Since when are you scared to get dirty?"

Tevin's devilish smirk tells all of our secrets. I give him a long, fluttering eye roll. "Your head is always in the gutter."

"What? I didn't say anything about sex," Tevin gasps and drops his jaw as if offended. The smile in his eyes gives away his playfulness. "That's you swimming in filth, ma'am."

Tevin proceeds to poke me in the middle of my forehead, and I, in turn, swat at his hand. "I am not a 'ma'am'!"

He fakes shock. "Excuse me for using manners."

I can't help but be amused by his silly ass. I snort, "Whatever, Tevin No-Campbell. I guess I can hang out with you for a little."

Hooking his arm around my shoulders, he pulls me toward his Jeep Wrangler, landing another age joke.

"Good, because I was about to say you're starting to move like somebody's grandma."

"You got one more time…!" I warn, jerking away.

I didn't get far, though. With a stretch of his long arms, he hooks me back again, tucking me under his armpit while mumbling apologies and sweet, nasty nothings. I giggle, knowing he'd fulfill each naughty promise and I'd let him every time.

Tevin and I created a picnic setting on the beach and watched the bright sun descend from high in the sky to the edge of the bay while we cleaned two takeout plates of smoked ribs, southern comfort sides, washing it down with a local beer. It wasn't until I drank my last drop of the tart IPA that I realized how much time had passed.

"I just know I have a mean tan right about now." Catching the last of the sun against my skin, I admire how it deepened my skin over the last couple of hours.

Tevin takes my outstretched arm and twists it as if he's examining it before he unexpectedly kisses the crook, then declares, "The darker the berry, the sweeter the juice."

Chewing on the inside of my lip, I bring my arm down and smize at his subtle flirt. I flirt back, "Well, you know, that is true. Ain't nothing gonna be sweeter than me."

"Mmm, you ain't never lied," he murmurs. Just as smooth as his previous gesture, he leans in and nips at my neck. My shoulders shrug in response to the ticklish sensation.

"Move, Tevin," I coo. I playfully push at him, but I don't really want him to go anywhere. "All you want me for is my body."

"Not true!" he quickly objects, his voice rising an octave. "If that were the case, I wouldn't have spent my check on this meal for you."

I tilt my head and move my eyes up to him. "Tevin, this meal ain't cost you that whole Fire Department check. Chill."

Tevin's eyes stretch as he props his arm on his leg. "Y'all really think firefighters rollin' in dough, huh?"

Not believing the scarcity he spoke of, I purse my lips at him. "You ain't broke. I wouldn't be dealing with you if that were the case."

"Damn, niggas stickin' me for my paper?!" Tevin grabs his chest dramatically, using the Biggie Smalls line to his comical advantage. His shenanigans send me into my signature laughing fit, clutching my chest as I wheeze. He continues his dramatics, straightening his back and pinning me with wide eyes and tight lips. "Damn, J, you gonna call all your homies with that squawk."

My laugh titters into a stuttering one as he looks up at

the circling seagulls and then back at me, meeting my narrow, offended eyes. His lips pucker, unable to hold in his amusement, and he breaks into his own howling laugh, falling back onto the sand.

I sit up on my knees and poke my finger into his chest, pouting, "That's not funny. I can't help the way I laugh."

Tevin's laughter doesn't cease as he warns, "Shit, you will if you don't want to call in killer seagulls and vultures and shit."

He tries to sit up, but I poke him in the chest again, pushing him back into the sand. "Seagulls don't kill people unless they pose a threat, bozo."

Tevin abruptly stops laughing, and his eyebrows deepen between his eyes. "Why would you know that, Joni?"

"Nova," I simply answer with a shrug. He releases a quiet "Oh," nodding his understanding. I shift the conversation back to our original topic. "Nah, for real. I'm not counting your money. I kick it with you because you're cool, ya know?"

"Yeah, I get it. You're cool, too…" Tevin's voice trails into a rasp, and his eyes soften in a way that makes my heart sputter and my breath shallow. Just as quickly as the moment came, it left as he blinked his eyes towards the bay. He returns them after a beat, accompanied by that devilish smirk again. "But, I really fucks with you because that box is *hot*!"

I gawk, totally not expecting him to say that in the moment, and for a moment, I can feel my heart deflating like a balloon pierced with a pin. I shake my head, internally brushing the feeling away and externally with incredulity of Tevin before I push at his chest again, knocking him down on the blanket we occupy. He lies there, still howling at my expense.

I collapse onto the side of my leg in a full pout as I fold my arms. In my peripheral vision, I see Tevin sit and then feel his arms wrap around my waist. I tug away, but not with much strength. That simple touch had my body tingling and wanting to succumb. He helps me do so by pulling me between his legs.

He works me over some more as he rasps in my ear, "Relax, I'm just playing." I untense my arms but still hold on to my pout as he continues, "For real, I fucks with you too because you're cool. I have fun when I'm with you and we talk about shit outside of the surface stuff."

He's nuzzled into my neck by the time he finishes his statement. His breath grows shallow, but with enough energy to be felt against the side of my neck. Goosebumps prick the area, and my insides turn to mush at the sensation. I narrow my eyes, still on the mission to feign away the effects of Tevin and focus my gaze on the crashing waves ahead of us and hum, "Mm-hmm."

"For real," he reiterates, his tone carrying a slight beg. He runs his fingertips down the side of my arm and then places them at my hips, giving them a slight squeeze. That squeeze is like a button, releasing all of the tension in my body. I lean into him, fully immersed in the moment. The way his voice remains mellow tells me he's doing the same. "Like right now, I've got something to tell you about work."

Curiosity stirs me, and I look over my shoulder, inquiring with my eyes. In his typical teasing fashion, he keeps his eyes trained on the waves ahead for a long beat, building the unnecessary anticipation. When he finally looks down at me, I'm wearing slits and an impatient pout that coerces a smirk from him before he looks ahead again. With a deep exhale, Tevin reveals, "Denzel wants me to man the Volunteer Squad."

"That's a good thing…right?" The sigh that drops after his confession makes me question the excitement that begins to fill me. I adjust so that I can dissect his face for clues. The corners of his mouth now droop, and his eyes are still straight forward, all telling me he's not as enthused as I thought he should be.

Sensing me looking at him, he moves his eyes back to mine and twists his mouth to the side. "Man, the volunteer squad is nothing but inexperienced goofs."

I felt the insult in his words, and I wasn't even one of the volunteers. I scoff, calling him out, "Oh, that's low, Tevin. You are literally still wet behind your ears yourself, you know?"

I bring my hand and tug said wet ear, and he jerks away, grimacing, "Aight, man, chill."

Tevin really isn't feeling my jokes from the screw of his face and the way he cuts his eye at me. I place my hands up as a sign of my surrender before wrapping my arms around his neck and pursing my lips, waiting for him to succumb to them. He eventually gives in and pecks my lips, but still holds a grimace. With satisfaction settling in my grin, I returned to my questioning, "For real, what's wrong with heading the Volunteer Squad?"

He sucks in a breath and pushes out, "The problem is, it's like them saying I can't handle managing a real squad. You know I've been wanting to be considered for a Captain role for a minute. It's highly likely that Denzel will move out of the chief position, and Deacon would take over, leaving the Captain spot open."

I nod, acknowledging his words. The odds of this really happening were high. With Nina about to pop and their nuptials approaching, I could see Denzel considering moving on to something more stable and less dangerous in the field.

Tevin continues, "We clown and joke all the time, but

right now, I feel like they really clowning me with this. I don't know if I want it."

"So, you'd rather stay stagnant than take on something new?" I ask, not seeing the logic in it, even with consideration of his feelings.

His frustration comes out in a huff as he admits, "Man, I don't know. It just feels like they're saying I'm 'inexperienced' or something." He makes quotation marks with his fingers before dropping his hands to his side and shaking his head.

"Tevin, *you are* the youngest in the crew," I point out. I'm very well aware he didn't want to be reminded, but in this moment, he needs the honest truth for my point to be made. "And with that fact, you are a little inexperienced. Maybe this is an opportunity for you to show them you know your shit. Spin that to make it work for you, Big Baby."

I knew the nickname at the end of my encouragement annoyed him. It was evident in the way his brows set between his eyes. I poke him in the chest and giggle, hoping he will lighten up and see the nickname as the joke that it really is, although, truthfully, he is like my Big Baby, young yet a big grown man at the same time.

Tevin's facial features have softened significantly by now. He clicks his tongue before admitting, "Aight, you might be right about spinning it to work for my good. I'll think about it."

"Good."

Content with our conversation, I return to my original position, my back against Tevin's chest, and his head nuzzled into my neck. I look to the bay waterline, where the sun was on its last few minutes of its descent. It's a peaceful view with the sky fading from a burnt orange to a maroonish color while the calm waves crash against the shoreline, and in the distance, I hear those "killer seagulls" squawking high in the sky.

I notice Tevin's fingertips grazing my arm and the breath it steals from my chest. It's these moments that our connection seems to teeter the line into something that feels more serious than what it is. I don't audibly question it; it's just something I ponder in my mind. In a corner of my heart, I feel like I don't want to bring awareness to it, fearing it will complicate things. We're fun and uncomplicated. That's how I like it.

Tevin breaks the silence that settles between us. "Ready to head out?"

I nod, and he helps me up from the sand before I fold our blanket and Tevin throws away our trash. Within a few moments, I head up the slight hill toward his truck with Tevin supporting my climb with his hand on the side of my glutes and his body close. In the brief moments that my bottom brushes against him, my arousal stirs, and I can feel his is too. When we reach his truck, he turns around, pulling me snug into him.

"Come here."

The command is rhetorical because there's no way we can get any closer, except for the connection of our lips. The way he angles his head down to mine, I know that's what he means and I lift on my toes and bring my head up to his, closing the final space between us. The kiss we share starts as a soft peck and then turns very sensual as he sucks on my bottom lip. It pulls a soft moan from me, giving him the entry to butterfly his tongue into my mouth. Oh, the butterflies that swim between my thighs. I wrap my arms around his neck and fully immerse myself in the tongue tangle.

"You know that 'Big Baby' talk always gets you in some shit," he murmurs against my mouth before dragging his tongue across my slightly pouty bottom lip. I flutter my eyes open to his piercing gaze, growing more brooding by the second. "It always has me thinking of ways to make you put some respect on my name."

He lets out a growling chuckle that sends a shiver down my spine. Oh, this man will have me spread-eagled out here on this cliff if I don't reel things back in. I slip from his grasp and giggle, playfully dismissing him, "Whatever, Tevin. Come help me into this truck."

Darkness takes over the sky now, with only highway lights illuminating over us. With a loose intertwining of our fingers, I lead him to the passenger side. He reaches over and opens the door for me. With his assistance, I hop into the Jeep. The simple gentleman gesture feels erotic as Tevin palms my backside and then slides his hand down my thigh. With a slight tug, he signals for me to face him. I do and he encourages my legs to part as he nestles between them.

The heat—oh, it's smoldering heat—permeates between us as he skates his fingertips up the side of my thighs and under the skirt of my dress, bunching it with each drag of it up my thigh. Feeling flustered, I tilt my head and flutter my eyes to his.

"Tevin…" His name comes out in breath that teeters between a whimper and a question as he finds the top of my panties and begins peeling them down. I'm not sure if I'm on the verge of begging him to stop or proceed. My body answers for me as my hips lift, assisting the thin material over the curve of my ass.

That reverberating growl takes over his throat again as he murmurs, "Mm-hmm, that's my name and I'm fittna make you wear it out…"

He works my panties down my thighs, and as he does, the soft, humid air creates a chill-inducing quiver to my dripping, now exposed center. Once removed from my legs, Tevin stuffs my panties into his khakis and then proceeds to loosen the top three buttons of his white button-up.

The preparation for what I know will be his devouring of my sweet peach is mouth-wateringly delicious to watch. Holding his focused gaze on mine as he gathers the bottom of my dress on either side. With a swift tug, he pulls me so that my bottom is nearly off the edge of my seat. A stiff gasp seeps from my parted lips, followed by body tremors at the abruptness and the anticipation. I try to mask how disheveled he has me with a nervous laugh and say, "Tevin, you are so-oooh…"

My words fail me the moment he dips his head between my thighs, attacking my swollen pearl with no warning. Instead, they crawl out of my open mouth as salacious moans as he goes to town on my pussy.

"I…love…this…shit…" I ooze, half-unknowing what's being panted out of me. The other half knows the declaration is all true. I love the spontaneity of us…of him. I've tried so many to not feel so satiated by this thing, but somehow the feeling always finds its way back in my bones by way of Tevin's choice of attachment to my lower extremities. Tonight, it's his head that stirs up this revelation, bobbing like the winning apple is the release gathering in my core.

I can't see what he is doing, but dammit, if I can't imagine every flip, every tap of his tongue that beckons my unravel. It's the best me toe-curling head to date—and I say that about every time he goes down on me. My toes curl tight, and I know I'm ruining my pedicure as my toenails carve my pleasure into the sole.

"Ahh..!" A throaty moan ascends from me as I throw

my head back. My eyes open to the stars twinkling through the open top, and I know my impending orgasm will send me into orbit with them. Gripping the edge of the seat with one hand and the headrest with the other, my legs begin to quake, my vision begins to blur, and I send a sinful praise as I rocket off, "Sweet, baby Jesus, Tevinnnnn…."

"Mm-hmm," he hums, the vibration causing my hips to spasm. "Say it for me one more time…"

"Tevin…!" I strain out as another convulsion tremors through me.

Tevin turns into a glutton at the sound of my offered praise, flattening his tongue and butterflying it between my walls. The feeling has my walls quivering again and again, and my vocals failing as my moan seeps out in a strained form as another wave crashes over me again.

It's this shit right here. The reason Tevin stays on speed dial when I'm in need. A Cookie monster with a monster, a deadly combination for my pussy—and she revives every time just to relive her same sweet demise again.

TEVIN

I would never need an alarm clock if Joni and I lived together. The snore coming from her little body sounds like one of those old-school riding lawnmowers you'd only find in your grandpa's backyard. It sounds like it's coming straight from her gut, loud and rumbling, like her engine is on its last leg. Shit, a couple of mornings, I found myself on my side, staring at her wondering where the hell she stored all that air and how she slept through it? Once, I caught her startle herself awake after cranking up her engine. It was the funniest shit because she popped her eyes open at me like I was the one snoring and disturbing her.

This morning, Joni's call for the hogs wakes me right as the sun cracks through the blinds of her room. Honestly, my body's been awake for about thirty minutes before she revved. Working 24-hour shifts often disrupts my body's natural sleep patterns, leading to inconsistent schedules. When it's up, it's up—just like my dick.

At six in the morning, my man is standing at attention and getting harder as Joni shifts in her sleep. It almost seems intentional how she keeps bumping her perfect bubble ass into me. With her last scoot, the way my rod is curved and pokes, I get a feel of the slickness puddled between her legs. I chortle, mentally trying to keep myself at bay, but when I peer down at her work of art, seeing how her chocolate mounds swallow up the little lace thong, I feel my willpower slowly dissolving.

I smooth my hand around her small waist and cup her teardrop breast. I love how her breasts form the shape, their fullness, and the slight droop of them. Cuddling up closer to her, I begin to massage the breast in my hand in an upward motion until I reach the point of her nipple. I repeat until her nipple stands erect, and I hear a faint moan from Joni.

"Tevin…"

"Good Morning," I growl, sinking my teeth into my bottom lip. Joni giggles and grinds her hips into me, causing my dick to ache with the want to feel her.

Leaving her taut nipple, I glide my hand down her hollowed stomach and trace the lace of her panties. She is warm to the touch, permeating a humid warmth that continues to confirm she's moist down there. My index finger traces a line down her middle as she spreads her legs open for me. Scissoring my fingers, I use one to pull her panties to the side and the other to explore her depth. She's so slick, it takes nothing for my finger to slip between her folds. I stroke her up and down, my finger drowning inside her. So, I add another.

"Mmm…" Joni grunts. It sounds muffled by the clench of her teeth on her lip. I keep working her, plunging in deep and slow with intentions to pull a full submission from her.

The way her walls grip my fingers with each plunge inside of her, I know I need to be deep inside of her. Removing my fingers, I wrap my arms around her midsection and pull her into me. Spooning her, I kiss up the curve of her shoulder, her neck, feeling and hearing her breaths quicken. Somewhere amid my kisses and kneading her ass, her hand grasping at my briefs, we end up with nothing between us but my rock-hard erection.

"Fuucckk…Joni…"

The force of my grunted words and the shudder of my body surprises the hell out of me. It collides with Joni's elongated moan, indicating my entry into her canal is just as pleasurable for her, too. She feels so fucking good, her walls clenching around my jimmy as I sink to balls deep.

I'd never tell Joni, but she has the best pussy I've ever had. Admitting it would be too much like me admitting she has me whipped, but the way I stay diving between her thighs, I probably don't have to say it. Her taste and the way her walls conform to me make me want to put a padlock on it.

"I fuckin' love this pussy, baby," I moan into Joni's ear with one hard thrust and her ass rippling against my thigh.

So much for keeping it to myself or keeping my composure. With each thrust, I feel her getting wetter.

How the hell can she get any wetter, I wonder, but only for a second. When she begins to throw back as I plunge inside her, static buzzes through my brain. My vision starts to blur. Joni's rousing moans are like music to my ears.

I can ride this wave all day, but my man is ready to tap out. The slap of our thighs, the squish of her juices… it all has my dick throbbing. My toes curl just as all of my blood rushes south. I grab hold of her breast as if it's my life support and go to pound town on that ass.

And then, Joni looks over her shoulder at me, brows furrowed and eyes holding a mix of lust and pleasure.

She is beautiful on the cusp of her climax.

God-damn beautiful Joni.

And just like that, it's game over.

"Tevin! Tevin!"

The pitch of Joni's voice is nothing like it was an hour ago. Then, it was soft and breathy before I knocked out like I'd lost a fight against Tommy Hearns. Now, she shrills, high and frantic, calling me like Debo stood outside her door. I blink a few times, trying to clear my vision and grab her arms to stop her from shaking me.

"What's up, Joni?" I ask, still in a daze.

"You gotta go. Nova is pulling up," she spits out. The fear evident in her almond-shaped eyes confuses me.

"Okay, and…?"

Joni's eyes widen as she shrieks, "What do you mean, 'and'? You can't be here when she gets up here!"

Joni bugs her eyes at me like I asked the dumbest question in the world. To me, it's a valid question. I hear about Nova all the time. What's so wrong with me finally meeting her? I don't have the chance to ask this because when I open my mouth to do so, Joni jerks away from my hold and pushes me off the bed.

My ass thudding on the ground is enough to knock the rest of the sleepy haze out of me and shocks me. Joni's really serious about me leaving. While I fumble my hands over the shards of clothing on the floor, she's zooming around the room in a panic. In a matter of moments, she's covering her naked body with her robe and swiping my clothes from the ground, shoving them into my chest like I'm some cheap floozy hanging around too long.

"Damn," I breathe, my face still stuck in disbelief at how quickly the energy has changed. Or maybe it hasn't changed, but has always been this way. Standing to my feet, I tilt my head to the side, asking, "Is it that bad of an idea that I'm still here?"

Having to ask already has my stomach cringing, because if I have to ask, that means it's always been a problem. By the time I finish, she's already at the bedroom door, and it hits me: She never had plans for us to meet.

Noticing I haven't moved beside twisting around to her, she sits on her hip and folds her arms, huffing, "Yes!"

With that single word, she swivels on the balls of her feet and swings the door open, continuing her haste.

"Why?" I question, following her out of the room, all while pulling my shirt over my head. "I don't see what the problem is. It's not like we're just fu—"

Joni spins, pinning me with wild eyes.

"Because she's not meeting somebody I'm just... fucking!"

She waves her hands around frantically, just as her words collide with mine. It leaves me with my jaw dropped, registering that we are on two different pages. That shit fucked my stomach up.

Joni must've realized the difference in our thoughts

of us, and her face softens. Her voice is smaller now as she tries to explain.

"You know what I mean, Tevin. We're not just… we…" Her face balls up along with her fists as she pinches her eyes shut, realizing she can't clear up what she said. There's no clearing it up. I see clearly what she's conveying.

Joni sighs, "Tevin, we can't go over this right now. I *really* need you to leave. She'll be here in like five minutes. Please."

"Say less."

I put my hand up, stone-faced. I see Joni silently gasp at my assertiveness.

She takes a few steps toward me.

"Tevin—"

"We good," I say, cutting her off. I didn't want her to say anything more. The dagger is already deep and twisted in my chest.

I walk back to her room to finish getting dressed, trying to mask the ridicule I feel. Here I am, looking like a real simp with my nose wide open and my eyes shut to the reality of the situation. Honestly, I thought I hadn't met her daughter yet because she's always with her dad when I come around. I pause in my steps when it all hits me: I'm only invited when Nova *is* at her dad's house. *Fuck, I really am just a lil' nigga she fucks.*

When I walk back through the living room, Joni tries

to stop me by placing her hands on mine. I avoid her eyes, looking over her head and to the door.

"Tevin, I'm sorry," she says, her voice mousy and small. When she realizes I have no plans to say anything, she tries again. "Seriously, I am…can we talk about this later?"

"Joni, we're good," I reiterate, this time with a little more bass in my voice as I move my narrow eyes down to her. She's giving me those puppy eyes and pouty lips. My chest dips for her, but I can't risk looking like a simp again. Her words skate through my head again.

"Because she's not meeting somebody I'm just… fucking!"

Taking in a stiff breath, I gently nudge her to the side. Laced with sarcasm, I mumble, "Let me go before she gets here. I'll see you around."

I halfway hope Joni will stop me from walking out, but when she doesn't, I don't stop either. I don't look back. I continue to trudge forward, feeling like the biggest slut walking the hall of shame.

Not really. But hearing Joni call me a fuck buddy in so many words makes a brotha feel cheap.

I make my way down to street level and hop into my Jeep, but I don't pull off right away. Instead, I sit there, listening to the caw of the seagulls and the purr of the engine, wallowing in my thoughts. My thoughts reveal it's more than just this situation with Joni that bothers me. It's everything, Joni and the Fire Department.

I don't understand why so many people doubt me as a man. First, it's my first family, and they have doubts about my ability to lead, which is why I'm in charge of the slackies in the Volunteer Squad. They didn't say that, but, c'mon, I'm essentially babysitting.

As if that's not enough of an ego blow, Joni's revelation is the gut-punch that knocks me on my mental ass. I at least thought Joni saw me as more than just some funny guy with a long dick, but this morning proved me wrong. She didn't even believe I was good enough to meet her daughter, let alone consider me a man she's dating.

A girl with two curly pigtails catches my attention from the driver's side mirror. She bops across the street to Joni's apartment complex. I couldn't see her face, but from her hair and the pictures I've seen, I knew it was Nova. My stomach hollows at the thought of how Joni doesn't think enough of me to let me meet her. With a final groan that deepens my sorrows, I sit there a while longer, making sure Nova enters the building safely before driving off, feeling smaller than I have in a long time.

TWO MONTHS LATER

TEVIN

"Lock & Key! What's good, my guys!"

I swagger into the fire station gym, finding Denzel and Deacon in the middle of a set. Even though they are the only two in the gym, it feels like the room is full of sweaty guys, even with the motorized steel garage door wide open.

As I approach, Deacon finishes his last chest press with Denzel helping him re-rack. They both look at me, clearly puzzled by the nicknames. I explain through a chuckle, "Yeah, I'm talkin' to you two chastity belt-wearing bums."

"Don't be mad because we have women who want to sleep beside us forever," Denzel jokes back, ambling over and dapping me.

"Yeah, loser," Deacon chimes in behind him. I look

past Denzel to Deacon, who is now sitting on the edge of the bench, wiping his face with a towel. He looks over to me. "From what I heard, you ain't got enough body to keep a woman warm at night."

I put my hands in front of me. "Pause, my guy. You worrying too much about my body when it's my dick that keeps your mama knockin' at my door."

To add more insult, I grab my dick and crudely shake it at him, laughing hysterically. Deacon hulks up and stomps towards me, but Denzel darts between us.

"Damn, y'all are like two big ass kids!" he fusses, placing a hand on Deacon's chest.

I watch Deacon huff and choose violence again.

"See, Denzel gets it. He knows I'm two pumps from being your step-daddy!"

I pump the air for emphasis, and Deacon falls prey to my antics, nostrils flaring like a bull as he grits, "Tevin, I'm gonna fuck your lil' ass up—"

His eyes turn to slits as he takes a step and whips his towel at me. I continue laughing while Denzel mumbles something, I'm sure, along the lines of him relaxing.

If I want to ruffle Deacon's feathers, all I have to do is mention Fallon or his mama—it works every time. That shit's funny to me mainly because, even though he's still a jokester himself, being married to Fallon has softened him, making it easy to get under his skin. I can admit, I probably showed up at the gym a little too fiery, considering it's only eight in the morning, but shit, it wouldn't be me if I didn't start some shit.

Feeling the energy settle, I extend a hand out to Deacon, calling for a truce. "Deac, you know I'm fuckin' wit you. It wouldn't be me if I didn't."

"And you know two things I don't play about: my wife or my Mama," he reminds. Still gritting at me, he moves in and daps me, closing it with a firm fist meant to cause pain.

"Aight, man," I say, jerking my hand away. I wring off the pain, but then smirk. "I feel you, though. I don't play about your Mama either."

A beat passes before Deacon catches on to my joke. When he does, his nostrils flare, that big ass vein pops from his neck, and I know he's two seconds from launching at me again. I quickly apologize, but continue to laugh at how easy it is to pull his strings. Deacon eventually lightens up and gives in to a dry chuckle before heading back to the weight rack.

Denzel and I follow behind, pre-empted with a playful warning from him. "One day, you're going to write yourself a check you can't cash, and I won't be here to keep Deacon from snapping your neck."

"Ehh, Deac knows my ass is full of jokes. Right, Deac?"

I lift my head and peer over my nose at Deacon through the mirror in front of us.

Deacon scowls but then smirks. "Yeah, that's why I don't break your little ass in two."

"Aight, man. You can't call me little anymore. I put on some weight."

I puff out my chest and flex, admiring the definition that cuts through my arms. If it weren't for my muscle shirt, my abs would be on full display. I knew the muscles were there, and they knew it too, despite how they started joking with me again, claiming they saw nothing. I brush it off, though. I'm not a swole barbarian like them, but I have lean muscle that catches the same amount of attention from the ladies.

Denzel goes through a set of curls before he finally gives me my props. "All jokes aside, I see you putting in work. You've been hanging tough with us still, even with your new responsibilities."

Knowing he's talking about the Volunteer squad, I cut my eyes and keep doing my set, mumbling, "Yeah, it's a lot of responsibility babysitting an eclectic group of volunteers," and then fuss, "Denzel, who chose this crew? I'm starting to think you're playing in my face."

I think back to one of my first drills with the squad. We were doing simple shit, like attaching the hose to a fire hydrant, and it was like I was teaching them rocket science. They've gotten better since then, but not by much. They still move like they have two left feet. Hell, one guy wears bifocals secured by tape. Every time I look at him, he reminds me of Damon Wayans in that movie, right before he turns into that goofy superhero Blankman.

Still, it felt like a losing battle with these volunteers, and it didn't help that the number of volunteers was dwindling. We started with ten recruits, and as of today, we are down to six; three of them I doubt will last much longer. Losing volunteers makes me feel like I can't do that job, which further reinforces my belief that I'll continue to be seen as someone they can't take seriously in leadership positions.

"We don't necessarily recruit," Denzel explains. "It's called a volunteer squad for a reason. Our local citizens volunteer, and we don't turn them down. You never know who may turn out to be a potential new member of our fire family. Look at you."

Deacon cracks up at my expense, and Denzel puts his hands up, signaling no harm meant. The damage was already done. I already feel like they've put me in an impossible position as a joke, and comparing me to them didn't help. I turn my focus to the whir of the fan and the hip-hop beat coming from the wall speakers as I pick up a weight and begrudgingly start my curls.

"I didn't mean it like that," Denzel insists. "But if we'd judged you by how small you were—or your maturity—we wouldn't have been able to see how much of an asset you are to the company."

Doing my last arm curl, I drop the weight, letting it clank against the steel rack. I turn to Denzel and Deacon, looking at them accusingly. "I might joke, but that doesn't mean I can't be taken seriously. That's what it seems, given that you've put me on the volunteer squad. And then you didn't even say anything, Deac."

"How did I get into this?" Deacon questions, bringing his hands up as he shrugs.

For the umpteenth time this morning, I twist my face at him in annoyance. "Because, you know, just as well as I do that when Denzel gets that call for District Chief, you're stepping in as Battalion, leaving the Captain position open."

"And you think you're supposed to get the Captain position?" Deacon folds his arms over his drenched company T-shirt, tilting his head towards me and lifting a questioning eyebrow.

I stare back, answering matter-of-factly, "Hell, yeah!"

Deacon laughs in my face, and my face grows hot. Denzel steps in and clarifies things once more. "I've said nothing about going District, *yet,* but even if I did, nobody has counted you out, but baby steps, Jedi."

Snorting, I question, "Baby steps? D, I've been in this company longer than any of these other cats, man."

Denzel walks over to me and squeezes my shoulder.

"Even more reason why I chose you to shape up the volunteer squad. Don't rush the process."

"Yeah, trust it, bro," Deacon enters the chat, stepping up beside Denzel. "Everybody's journey is different. Ain't nothing wrong with leading The V-Squad. Build your leadership muscles like you're trying to build those chicken wings of arms."

"I got your wings." I attempt to put Denzel in a head-lock, but he peeps my angle and dips under my arm to only stand up and place me in a headlock.

"Aight, Deac! You play too much!"

"Nah," he says, tightening his grip. "Tell me. What's that you say about my mama?"

"*How many ways I love you…*"

Hitting a two-step and then bumping my hip into the door, I push the storefront door shut, assuming it closed entirely behind me. I couldn't hear anything but the music blaring through my Beats earbuds as I finished my duet with Toni Braxton. Today, she's my background singer while I hit all her ad-libs as I prance around the empty boutique room of Love x Lace. I'm sure the notes I belted out were probably off, but in my head, I hit every high and signature low note with ease. All I care about is the good mood this '90s bop puts me in before turning brides into baddies.

The song has a catchy groove, making it easy for one to fall into a nice hip roll in the middle of a two-step. It feels like summertime, cookouts, and love. The lyrics help with the latter feeling, with her crooning about how many ways she could love her man. If a man had you counting the ways you can show him you love him, he had to be a good man. An Aaron Pierre "That's Mufasa" kind of man. I found myself sipping a little too hard on the straw of my iced coffee, thinking about Aaron Pierre, and giggling at myself. I don't know what has gotten into me, having an eye for these younger men.

I sigh and place my iced coffee onto the counter before heading to the back of the boutique to put away my personal belongings, thinking about the one particular young man I can't seem to get rid of—well, at least it seemed that way a month ago. I haven't spoken to Tevin since he left my apartment, minutes before Nova arrived. I can still see the disappointment on his face; hell, my heart still cringes at the thought of it. It was awkward and foul how it went down, but he knew what it was! Tevin and I haven't been doing anything but fucking around since we met over a year ago. We have fun—lots of it. And even though we do have great chemistry, we've never been anything else but…friends with benefits—even though it feels like there could be more than that between us. Still, with all of the grey area, and Nova, I didn't feel like I was there to let him meet her.

Nova Skye Banks isn't quite a baby anymore. She's eight going on eighteen, if you ask me, but still, she's my baby. It's been just me and her for the most part over the last five years, after her dad and I split. Since then, I've been focused on ensuring the transition to sharing time between me and her dad went smoothly for her. With her challenges, I didn't want my stuff and her dad's stuff to be another obstacle for her, nor did I want the addition of a man I wasn't seriously dating to be around for her to get attached to. That's why Tevin couldn't stay. We weren't serious, and we never discussed it, despite the undeniable connection we seemed to have. The way Nova reads people, she'd be reading into things more than she needed to.

Thinking of Nova, I grab my phone out of my purse before I lock it up, tapping to open the Lovey's Bay School System's Parent Portal. It was nearing nine-thirty, and she should've just finished her session with her IEP Teacher. Just as I suspected, she did, and there was a message from her teacher for me.

Ms. Morrison,

Nova is making great progress, despite how hard she is on herself. Please continue to encourage her not to rush through her reading, but to take her time. She will speed up at the perfect time!

Miss Shelby

I release a thoughtful sigh, imagining Nova's little face balling up while she fidgeted with her glasses because she was frustrated with her trouble with reading. I'm always telling Nova that there's no right speed when it comes to reading and that she's comprehending what she's reading better by taking her time, but my girl is a determined one. She understands she has a little more challenge with reading and comprehension because of her diagnosis of dyslexia. She refuses to let it hinder her. When words fail her, she draws. And because it takes her a little more time to comprehend, she listens impeccably —probably too much, because if I'm not careful, she could recite a whole conversation I'd spoken with Nina. And when reading gets too stressful for her, she turns to audiobooks. She loves listening to stories, especially fantasy, which is probably why my girl is a little drama queen with a big imagination. One day, I'm going to enroll her in acting classes so she can put her skills to use.

Making a mental note to discuss the message with Nova later, I shift my thoughts to the day ahead at Love x Lace. I'm thankful that the store will be in my hands and my hands only, as the owner, Lorna, is off today. I wish that Lorna would act like other owners and stay at home, but I get it, Love x Lace was her baby.

Love x Lace is the premier bridal boutique in Lovey's Bay, known for one-of-a-kind gowns from all over the country, with some flown in from overseas, thanks to Lorna's fashion connections. We're the number one stop for bridalwear, thanks to me. Yeah, I'm tooting my horn. I am that girl. That number one on the sales chart, and it's no surprise to me. I like to have fun, make the brides laugh, and I gas them up in everything they put on—that looks good, that is. That's another thing about me, I'm not going to sugarcoat shit for a sale. If you don't look good in the dress, I'll tell you and then help you find something that suits you better.

My expertise and overall character are what helped me secure the store manager position at Love x Lace, and I thoroughly enjoy every moment of being in the role. I like running the show, and for the most part, Lorna lets me do my thing without interfering. Lately, however, she's been on one. Ever since Tinsley McCoy, now Lennox, Greenbooks' superstar, purchased her wedding dress from Love x Lace, we've received numerous new inquiries. So many that our books are solid a year out from now. Tinsley didn't actually come into the store; her stylist, Kennedy Belafonte, did, but it didn't matter to the brides, just as long as they had the opportunity to shop where Tinsley did.

Albeit busy, it wasn't anything I couldn't handle, which is what I told Lorna. What makes us special is that we specialize in true upscale boutique service. We typically have at most two brides in the boutique at a time, allowing them to receive undivided attention and assistance from one of our two consultants working that day, with me being one of them. Now, though, we have an additional consultant for a day or two when I need to handle some administrative work.

After settling in, I strut from the back like I own the place, earbuds in, and nearly run into Whitney, my favorite consultant.

"Oh, shit, Whitney! You can't be popping up like that!"

I saw her mouth moving, but I couldn't hear anything over the music in my earbuds. Fumbling with my phone, I manage to tap the music off to listen to her chuckle and repeat, "I didn't pop up. I've been here for fifteen minutes now."

"Well, why didn't you say something?" I ask, pulling the earbuds from my ears and placing them in their case. I walk past her, tucking my phone and buds in the drawer under the register.

"Would you have even heard me, though?"

I look over my shoulder at Whitney, who was pinning me with a look that said she was right about her rhetorical question. Shrugging, I snort, "You're right. I was jamming, girl!"

"Oh, I know. When I walked in, you were running some rifts like you were Phony Braxton or something."

Tapping the last number and successfully signing myself into the system, I twist around on the balls of my heels, glaring, appalled. "I know you ain't talking, fake Baby Whitley."

Whitney guffaws, "Oh my God. How many times do I have to tell you I do not look like Jasmine Guy?"

"Bitch, you look like Jasmine Guy."

I folded my arms, pursing my lips at her, and she let out an exasperated groan before we both laughed. She throws her hands up, surrendering to the fact that she indeed looks like Jasmine Guy. I didn't know why she fights it. It's a resemblance she'll never get away from. I'm even convinced she's lying when she says her mother isn't her. If she wasn't, Whitney is a young doppelganger of her. She has fair skin, strong, high cheekbones, and thin, mildly plumped lips, just like her. What tops off the resemblance is that she wears her hair in a flowing roller set, similar to Jasmine Guy's Whitley character from A Different World, in season five. She's petite, too, and always wears fashion-forward dresses or suits in white or black, as per our dress code, giving all the prissy Whitley vibes. Barely thirty, Whitney is remarkably mature for her age and exudes a confident, "I-know-what-I-want" persona, adding even more to the cunning similarity.

Whitney and I continue with our usual banter as we open the boutique with expectations of our ten o'clock brides arriving shortly. Just off the strength of how well we carried on from me joking about her twinning with my favorite college student to business, easily made her my favorite and best consultant. We just vibed. We had the same sense of humor, and she loved the job as much as I did. Rarely did we ever have a day when none of our brides left without saying yes to a dress. We'd easily seal the deal on our own, or if it looked like we might have an undecided bride, we'd tag-team to bring her over to the winning side. Works every time.

This morning, it looked like neither of us needed an alley-oop from the other. By the end of our first two-hour session, Whitney celebrated her client's choice in dress with the ring of the store's handbell, a quick selfie, and a promo video for our social media.

Feeling the luck surrounding me, I turn away from the celebratory scene and strut over to the area where my client, Davina, is modeling her dress. She's a cute, small-framed girl and looks no more than her mid-twenties. I watch her twist her hips left and right, the big tulle skirt of the royal princess-style dress stiffly swaying. Her two friends, a guy and a girl, along with the person whom she introduced to me as her brother, watch with interest.

"Joni, what do you think?" she timidly asks, looking away from the mirror and over her shoulder to me. Her tone holds uncertainty, but the way her eyes gloss over and her smile beams, I knew she already had the answer to the question she posed to me.

I saunter over to the round stand she stands on,

running my fingers over the appliqués as I eyeball each one until my eyes meet hers. I smirk as I respond, "Looks like you already have the answer, boo."

She bites her lip, trying to hide her smile as she squirms and whines, "Joniii, but I need to know from you. What do *you* think?"

This is the type of relationship I typically build with all my clients. Within the two-hour session, I bond with them in a way that they seek my every piece of advice, as if we've been best friends for years. It's not done solely for a sale; I'm just a social butterfly like that. It just happens to end in a solid sale, as I knew this one would. I stop walking when I'm standing in front of her, and her crew is positioned behind her like an audience to my judgment call. Her friends look at me, wide-eyed, too, while her brother peers at me with an intriguing smirk that seems to cross his face every time we make eye contact.

I focus my gaze on Davina and cross my arms. "Well, if you want my honest opinion..." I pause for the dramatics and look her up and down again. When I met her eager eyes once more, they were bigger than saucers. Beaming at her, I declare, "Honey, you are wearing this dress! You're going to look like royalty walking down the aisle. Queen Bey, who?!"

"Eeek! I knew it!" Davina squeals and shimmies

again. She looks over her shoulder. "Avery, this is the one!"

I move my eyes to the silent yet not hard-to-miss man who responds to the name. His name is easy on the ears, and he's even easier on the eyes. His resting smirk turns into a proud and charming smile as he nods to her, replying with no hesitation, "You got it, baby girl."

Davina and her friends erupt into a chorus of squeals and conversation as they gather around her. I feel like a proud auntie, grinning at the sight, before walking around them, leaving them to celebrate. Avery meets me halfway, his gait relaxed and full of confidence, with his hands in his gray slacks. The closer he gets, the more I can see just how handsome he is.

"I guess it's time for me to find out my damage, eh?"

Avery's debonair smirk takes over his full lips again as he raises a dark, thick brow. His lips part slightly, revealing pearly white teeth, perfect against the cinnamon color of his skin. This man is fine, and I know he's aware of it. Thankfully, he couldn't see that I am well aware of his attractiveness. I purse my lips in a cool, modest grin, as I agreed, "It does seem about that time."

I tilt my head in the direction of the register and lead the way, swaying my hips with each step. I can sense him watching me and bite on the inside of my lip to maintain my composure as I take my place behind the register to face him. Avoiding the temptation to look at him again, I tap on the tablet screen, pulling up Davina's dress choice.

"So, with the dress and all of her accessories, you're looking at…" I swivel the screen in his direction, revealing the five-figure total. This is when I lift my eyes over his six-foot-something frame to study his facial expression, looking for a hint of discontent.

There was none.

His smile remains intact as he reaches into his pocket and pulls out a slender billfold. With a quick retrieval, he passes me a shiny gold card between his fingers.

"This should cover it, Ms. Morrison."

I retrieve the card and twist my mouth into a grimace.

"Call me Joni. Got me in here feeling like some-body's auntie."

Avery's laugh rumbles through the air. "How do you think I feel? I'm paying for my little sister's wedding gown, and I haven't walked an aisle yet."

My eyebrow piqued slightly at the reveal that he is single. Swiping his card, I chuckle, "I'm sure your lady will be hinting for you to put a move on it soon."

He shifts so that he's leaning against the counter, sending his spiced cologne wafting to my nose. "I have to find one first."

I move my eyes up to him. His gaze and his heart-throbbing smile burn through me. There was no missing it—he's flirting with me. Feeling tongue-tied, I continue with my task, and in seconds, I'm closing out the sale.

Chuckling away my nerves, I slide him the receipt and pen, instructing, "If you could sign right here."

With a quick loop and swipe, Avery signs his signature. Just as he readies to pass me the receipt back, he pauses, going back into his pocket. He pulls out a thick cream-colored business card and combines it with the receipt and pen, placing them all in my hand. I look down at the card, reading his name and phone number in cursive print.

"Perhaps, I can take you out one day. You know, put in some effort to meet my 'lady' one day."

There I was again, nerves rattling and cheeks blushing. I haven't gotten this nervous around a man in so long. Hell, I didn't really make myself that available to have men openly flirt with me like Avery is doing now. The one time I put myself out there was last year when Fallon and I attended the speed dating event at Rhythm & Brews. Even then, the chance to mingle with new men ended up being cut short because Tevin and I matched. This is different. There was no man around to cockblock, just a tall, brown, gorgeous man who swiped his card with no hesitation, flirting with me.

I didn't have time for it, though.

"Maybe," I answer, sliding the receipt into the

register drawer and tucking his business card in the drawer underneath.

With a slight defeat in his chuckle, he nods to me. "I'll take that. It was nice meeting you, Ms. Mor—Joni. And thank you for the superb service with my sister."

"Absolutely," I say, giving him a polite smile before he strolls away. Whitney took his place soon after.

"He's cute," she coos, wiggling her eyebrows.

"Yeah, he is," I admit, trying to sound as apathetic as possible. "He gave me his card, too."

Whitney's face lights up as she quietly gasps.

"Oooh, do I smell a summertime fling?"

She leans over the counter with both elbows with more excitement than I. I twist my lips to one side, confirming, "Girl, no. When Nova leaves for the summer, all I want to do is do me, catch up on some sleep…maybe get a little sun."

"Bor-ing!" Whitney quips. "Let me find out you're about to be that little old lady living in a shoe…that's how the nursery rhyme goes, right?"

"First of all," I start, snaking my head at the comparison. "There will be no slander that begins with 'old' coming my way."

"Well, if you weren't acting like you're 75 instead of 35…" she murmurs, earning herself a playful shove.

"I am not acting like that, I just…I don't know…"

My thought is cut short as Davina and Avery walk

out of the showroom with her crew behind them. I'm thankful for the interruption because I didn't have a solid answer to give Whitney on why I'm not eager to pursue the obvious interest Avery has in me. I round the counter and meet Davina, who pulls me into a hug as soon as she can wrap her arms around me.

"Thank you so much, Joni. I couldn't have done this without you…or my brother." She smirks and looks over her shoulder at Avery, who nods and smiles at me.

I pull back and deadpan at her. "Oh, you could've, but I don't know if you would've gotten the Joni effect—so… I guess not!"

I laugh at myself, and she joins in before leaning in and saying, "I think Avery fell for the Joni effect too, but don't tell him I told you that."

Davina squeezes my hand before prancing out of the boutique like the princess she is, leaving me wondering if I should add a tall, dark, and handsome man to my summer bucket list.

● **3**

TEVIN

The soft, melodic sound of wind chimes nudges me from my sleep, starting as a gentle whistle. Eventually, as I coast into being fully awake, the whistles turn into loud bongs of metal hitting metal. I blink slowly, and with each blink, I adjust to the darkness of my room. I face the sun-blocking curtains, which are still effectively blocking the four o'clock sun.

I only know the exact time because I set my alarm to go off at that specific moment, helping me stay productive on days off after a 24-hour shift. Before taking on the Volunteer Squad, my day off would consist of being in bed all day, flicking through the channels, and binging whatever food I could order from the GrubSpot app. Now, my off days aren't so lazy. I have to stick to a schedule to ensure everything is done.

After letting the alarm trill for a second time after pressing snooze, I finally started moving. Reaching across the cool, empty side of my bed, I tap the lit screen on my phone and turn the alert off before rolling out of bed. With my eyes now adjusted to the darkness, I walk to the window, pull the curtains wide open, squinting at the bright contrast.

"Shit," I groan, blinking to adjust to the daylight. "Probably wasn't the best idea."

The sun isn't high in the sky, but at a perfect angle, where I know the temperature is comfortable for some of the household errands I want to complete today. On my schedule today, there's yardwork and some laundry. With my to-do list on my mind, I turn and see one other task staring at me.

I smirk and open my arms wide.

"Frenchie, baby!"

Francheska, also known as "Frenchie", tilts her head and looks at me, almost like she's answering me. I chuckle and squat down, scooping her under my arms. "I know my bitch gotta pee. C'mon."

Frenchie squirms beneath my hold, but only to get comfortable as I scratch the top of her head. With an energized pep in my step, I head to the bedroom door. When I swing open the door, the smell of bleach and lemon smacks me in the face. It's so strong, I know my nose hairs are disintegrating. Frenchie squeaks out a whimper.

"I know, French," I tell her. "That nigga never holds back on the bleach."

With a quick rub to her head, I jog down to the stairs to the first level, finding Jace spraying the counter with a cleaning solution, which I'm sure includes more bleach.

Sensing my presence, Jace glances over his shoulder at me as I approach.

"What up, Tev."

"The toxicity level," I state, scrunching my nose. "Man, you do realize you're not supposed to mix bleach and other cleaning products, right?"

He sucks his teeth and keeps wiping down the counter, muttering, "I only used a capful."

"You sure about that?" I quiz, chuckling as I walk out of the room towards the living room, seeking fresh air. When I turn around, Jace is not too far behind, his lips tight and brows crinkled with slight guilt.

"Maybe... I used a little more than a capful. My bad, Clarke."

I chuckle at his confession. "It's all good. We'll survive today." I turn to continue towards the back door, but stop and point at him.

"And it's Tev or Tevin when we're at home, my guy. Loosen up."

I catch Jace's nod before I pull open the back door,

letting Frenchie out to roam and relieve herself in the backyard. Bleach aside, I can't lie—I'd rather have a roommate who cleans than doesn't.

Princeton "Jace" Carter has been staying with me for the past month, and I knew he was still adjusting to life in every way. While many of the volunteers at the V-Squad were doing it purely out of interest in being helpful citizens of Lovey's Bay, volunteering was a bit more of a requirement for Jace. After spending five years in prison immediately after his eighteenth birthday, doing volunteer work was part of his probation conditions. Choosing to volunteer with Lovey's Bay Volunteer Squad was his decision, driven by his interest in fire-fighting and a desire to build a new reputation.

I couldn't help but raise an eyebrow when Denzel told me about his past and that he was between homes. First, he'd been locked up for armed robbery.

"*Accessory* to Armed Robbery," I remembered Denzel clarifying. "Which means he didn't perform the robbery, just drove the getaway car."

We were in Denzel's office that day, about a week after I'd started working with the volunteers. Jace had opened up to him about his situation, and being the caring nigga that he is, Denzel offered to help him find somewhere stable to stay.

I remember scoffing at Denzel's attempt to downplay

the seriousness of his charges, retorting, "I hear you, D, but you're springing this all on me and then asking me to let him stay in my crib. I don't know the little guy from a can of paint, and you're telling me he was part of a robbery."

"I understand your concern. Really, I do," Denzel assured, sitting on the edge of his desk. "But, his probation officer says he's not the kind of guy his charges paint him out to be. He was just a kid when it all went down, hanging out with the wrong crowd…you know how the story goes. He took the fall, and now he needs a hand up."

Even with Denzel vouching for him, I was still leery, but what kept me from declining was seeing Jace put in the work with the squad. He's a team player with the potential to lead, which is what revealed his true character to me. Although he wears a permanent straight face on most occasions and is built like 50 Cent, he didn't have the rapper's ego. He was quiet, dedicated, and kept his head on straight. So, here he is, my temporary roommate, cleaning and cosplaying as Geoffrey from The Fresh Prince.

After watching Frenchie for a few minutes, I turn around, finding Jace sitting on the arm of the couch after unwrapping the cord for the vacuum. He looks up at me and sighs, "Some habits are hard to kick. I used to always try to keep my cell clean, so, you know. I see this as a way to show my gratitude for letting me crash here, knowing—"

"Hey, man," I say, raising my hand. "You said you want to be seen as a different guy, right? Drop your old story and start telling your new one. Got it?"

I dip my head, keeping stern eyes on him. Jace is hesitant to smile, but he does and nods his understanding. "You're right. But I'm still going to finish vacuuming. It's the least I can do after leaving popcorn crumbles on the couch and floor."

I start lifting my feet as if hot coals were underneath them, scanning the floor and noticing yellow specks of kernels buried in the carpet and on the couch. "Ugh! Yeah, get to vacuuming, man!"

Jace chuckles and says, "I told you," as I walk past him.

Although still something to get used to, I kinda enjoyed having another human in the house. Frenchie was cool, but I can only have so many conversations with a dog. The house and life have gotten quiet and a little lonely after I decided to step back from Joni. It's only been a month, but the silence and emptiness from not hearing her voice or seeing her face have felt like it's been months. Jace's arrival came at just the right time, giving me little room to overthink my decision to stop being Joni's fuck boy and focus on other things. I retrieve my laptop from the nightstand, place it on the freshly made bed, and open it to one of the things I've been focusing on: Fire Science.

The idea of pursuing my Associate's Degree in Fire Science crossed my mind before, but after joining the Volunteer Squad, I felt I needed something to prove I should be taken seriously. Credentials tend to change how people view you, and earning my Associate's Degree would be solid proof that I deserve serious consideration for a role like Captain. Many firefighters went after the degree when aiming for positions like lieutenant or captain, making it a logical choice. Luckily, I caught the last part of the enrollment period for classes starting in the Fall. Registration closed in a few days, and all I needed to do to secure my spot was handle the financial part. That's what I planned to do today.

Just as I completed my payment, an email notification slid across my screen.

VOLUNTEER SQUAD: Weekend Bridal Shoot Assignment - Fire Watch Duty

I click on the notification, curious about the details in the email sent by Denzel. I silently curse and snort as I read through the short message:

Tevin,

Heads-up on a new assignment for the squad:

There's an engagement bridal photoshoot sched-

uled for this weekend on Lovey's Bay Beach—Saturday afternoon, weather permitting. Love x Lace Bridal Boutique will be there with the bride, and the photographer is requesting fire presence due to elements like torches and sparklers being used. This is an excellent opportunity for a few volunteers to get their feet wet.

Contact for Love x Lace is Joni Morrison, who will be on site. Oh, and the bride...it's my baby. You know how much of a fire hazard she is. I'm trusting you to keep her safe!

Let me know if you need anything.

—Chief Peyton

"Ain't this some shit..."

I roll my eyes up toward the ceiling, sarcastically laughing at the circumstances. My laugh settles, but my cheeks ache, clueing me in on the smile that's plastering my face. I groan, low-key disappointed at how my heart is betraying me. Even when I want my heart to stay blue, stoned, and cold, the simple thought of crossing paths with Joni tempts it to thaw and beat warm again.

JONI

"Nova Skye..."

I give the simple chicken and red sauce pasta two stirs before glancing over my shoulder at Nova. I assume she didn't hear me call her with the fuchsia headphones covering her ears as she sits at the dining table, drawing on her iPad. I smirk, choosing to let her be lost in her imagination for a few more minutes while I let the quick meal simmer. This decisive thought collides with the loud buzz of my phone vibrating across the counter. I tap in the call and cradle the phone between my shoulders and ear.

"Hello."

"Hey, girl. What are you doing?" Nina greets with her usual melodic tone.

After topping the pan with a lid, I switch the phone

call from speaker to my earbuds, stating, "I just finished making dinner for me and Nova."

"Oo, what's for dinner?"

"Something slight. I made a quick chicken pasta."

Nina hums, "Mm, sounds good. You'll have to share your recipe."

I pause from wiping down the counter and look at the invisible camera. "Now, Nina…"

"Joni, stop!" Nina cackles. "Stop trying to steal my joy and help a girl out. I have a whole family to feed now."

I continue to wipe down the spot while letting my laughter simmer. "You're right. It's not just Denzel who has to suffer now. There's Aidan, too."

"Joni!"

I couldn't help teasing Nina. Although Nina isn't the walking fire hazard she was when she met Denzel, she still struggles with cooking. Tevin would often joke about how the crew clowns Denzel for his "struggle meals" prepared and packed by Nina. Shit, at least my girl is trying, but now that she has a new baby in the family, I need to stop laughing and help my girl learn how to make digestible food.

"I'm just picking with you," I assure her. I check the aromatic pasta, and my stomach pangs at the delicious smell. Opening a cabinet to grab some plates, I say, "I got you on the recipe, and I'll even walk you through your first try. I gotta make sure my godbaby and brother-in-law will survive the next 18 years."

Nina's pout can be heard through a short huff over the line. I stifle my laughter to save her feelings and shift the subject to Aidan and her recovery.

A few days after Fallon and Deacon's surprise wedding, Nina had a surprise of her own: the birth of Aidan. It wasn't really a surprise. Her belly was round and sitting low, and she was also nearly a week past her due date at the time of the wedding. Aidan eventually decided he was ready for the world, making his arrival a few days later.

"It's a lot with a new baby, but I feel good!" Nina explains, her voice a bit shaky, but confident. "I'm glad I'm out of the woods with my doctor, just in time for my engagement shoot. It's going to be so much fun!"

A calendar flashes through my mind, emphasizing this Saturday as Nina talks. "Oh yeah, it is this week. Explain to me again, why are you playing with fire after all your mishaps?"

Nina's annoyance is clear in her sigh, and I murmur an apology before she answers, slightly offended, "I don't care what my experience with fire used to be. I've been delivered and saved by my Love from my fear of all things fiery and smoky. Besides, the optics will be super cute on camera: me in a wedding dress, Denzel in the background with his fire uniform, and the blow torch shooting off fire while I blow it away. Tell me, it's not a dope idea!"

I agree, still with skepticism hidden in my tone, "It does sound pretty dope. Thankfully, you were smart enough to buy a cheap wedding dress for this idea, in case something goes wrong."

"Aht! Aht! Aht! Don't speak those things over my shoot! Besides, Denzel said the Volunteer Squad will be on site, *just in case*. I don't think there will be any problems, though."

My jaw slacks at the mention of the volunteer squad, bringing Tevin to mind. "Oh, yeah?"

"Yeah. Their volunteer squad is up and running now. Did you know Tevin is the lead for them? He should be there."

I don't tell her that Tevin talked to me about the opportunity a while back. I don't say anything.

Why didn't he tell me he decided to take on the gig?

"No, I didn't know," I finally respond, leveling my tone so that she can't hear my disappointment.

It's been two months with this awkward silence between Tevin and me. No calls. No texts. Just radio silence on both ends. I hadn't reached out because I didn't know what to say after our last exchange. He left me with a dry, emotionless "We good." How was I supposed to respond after that? So I didn't. I waited for him to initiate, but he didn't. Apparently, we aren't as good as he stated.

I could hear Nina continue to ramble on about the volunteer squad and Tevin, but I'm still reeling, mentally, feeling left out of Tevin's milestone. My ears perk when she says, "Oh, and I'm so proud of him for deciding to further his education."

"What?"

My words come out an octave higher than I want and breathy as I blink hard. There's a pregnant pause on Nina's side of the phone before she reiterates, "Yeah, Denzel said Tevin's enrolling in classes for his Associate's Degree in Fire Science. Looks like our boy is growing up!"

I have to place my hands on the counter behind me, because I feel like the rug has been jerked from under my feet. I stare at nothing but see just how disconnected Tevin and I really are right now.

Why wouldn't he share any of this with me? I'm never left out like this.

The realization hollows my stomach. Maybe we aren't good. Hell, we aren't even 'okay' if you ask me.

I can't be mad. I literally ostracized him from a part of my life. What do I expect?

The thought volunteers its space in my mind as my words to Tevin from our last encounter run through my head. I meant what I said, but not how it came out. I wasn't ready for Nova to meet Tevin, especially not in the state we were in that morning. I didn't want her to meet a man I was just having a good time with. What does that say to her? And even if that said man makes me feel things that aren't just "feel good" feelings, I wasn't ready for the step, for many reasons.

"That's what's up," I finally push through a breath, simultaneously pushing away my turmoil of thoughts.

"Yeah, it is," Nina drags out, evident that she's trying to decipher me. "You didn't know, did you? I'm surprised. That's your boo thang."

A half smile settles on the corner of my mouth as I blink down at my red-painted toes. "I mean…we're cool. It doesn't mean I know *everything* going on with him."

"Hmm," Nina hums. Her end of the line grows silent for a second, be she doesn't reveal her unspoken thoughts. Instead, she says, "Okay. If you say so. But I have to go. Baby boy will be hungry any minute now. See you Saturday?"

I nod my head as if she could see me. "Yeah. See you then."

After quick goodbyes, I tap my earbud to end the call. A smaller voice chimes, giving away how nosey she had been.

"Who's cool, Mommy?"

I look up, meeting Nova's big, round eyes. She's still sitting at the dining room table, and her head is cocked to the side as she wiggles her eyebrows curiously. The pink headphones are still over her ears, but her particular question had my eyes narrowing at her obvious ear hustling.

"Nobody, nosey," I respond and then purse my lips. "If you heard that, I know you heard me calling you moments ago."

She sits up straight in her chair, answering quickly, "I didn't. My audiobook just finished."

"Mm-hmm," I hum and snicker, half-heartedly believing her story.

I believe she was listening to her audiobook at one point, but I wholeheartedly believe she also listened in on my conversation. I walk around the island, separating the kitchen from the dining area of our apartment. When I approach Nova, I gently tug at one of her curly pigtails before sitting in the chair beside her, moving on to a more appropriate topic.

"Speaking of books, Ms. Shelby checked in with me today."

Her auburn eyes dim slightly at the mention of Ms. Shelby as she drops them down to her now dark iPad. She confesses, "I couldn't get it today, Mommy."

The disappointment in her words and face makes my heart twist and pang, and I place my hand on her little balled-up fist, squeezing it. "What do you mean, baby?"

"I couldn't find my words...I couldn't find the

words…" She struggles to explain. She squeezes her eyes shut and then blows her cheeks out. "I was too slow today, Mommy. I hate when I'm slow."

"Nova…"

I scoot my chair so that I am closer to her and wrap my arm around her tiny frame. Her body becomes heavy as she lays her head on my bosom, her shoulders drooping simultaneously. I move my finger under her chin so that she looks at me.

"Remember the story I told you about how I named you, baby girl?"

Her sad eyes stretch slightly as she nods. The way she looks at me has my eyes misting. Her big almond eyes widen, so wide the whites show while her irises reflect her innocence, just like the first time she ever looked at me. I rub her shoulder with my thumb as my mind drifts back to the moment I named her.

"When the nurse placed you in my arms, stars filled my eyes and then my heart. It was like seeing that I caught my own shooting star when you were placed in my arms. That's when I told your Daddy, "Her name is Nova Skye." That's because you are the brightest of them all, baby girl. You are bright. You are smart. Don't ever let anyone dim your light, not even yourself."

She pouts, "Mommy, I just don't like when my words jumble up. It makes it hard for me. Then I can't think.

The words weren't right when I was reading, and I kept getting them wrong, Mommy. Why can't I just be normal?"

She sniffles through her frustration and pinches her eyes closed again. I blink away the tear that threatens to drop before I tap Nova's third eye. She moves her eyes to me. I lift my head, but my narrowed eyes look down at her.

"Baby girl, to be normal is boring. You have a super-power. You know that?"

The corner of her lips twitches left to right as she attempts to hide her impending smile. She drags out, "Yes…"

I continue, "…and with superpowers, you do things differently. You do things *your* way. You have to read a little slower? Okay, you get to be in the world of your book longer. Your mind jumble up the words when you read? That means you have the power to create some-thing different…dare I say…better?!"

My voice goes up an octave, and I shimmy my shoul-ders. Nova begins to brighten again, just like the star she is. Her giggle swells my heart, and I find relief in her smile.

Sitting tall, I place my fists on my hips and snake my head, affirming, "You are Supa Nova, baby! Say it back!"

She mimics me, head-snake and all, and screams, "I'm Supa Nova!"

Our laughter collides as I pull her into my lap and give her the tightest hug. I rock her from side to side and breathe out, letting my eyes drift shut, thankful to be able to brighten my shining star yet again. This is a regular routine, where Nova's learning disability gets her down, and I reel her back in. At first, it was really hard on both of us. For her, the struggle to learn without being frustrated, and for me, it just hurts to see my baby girl hurt. It wasn't until I remembered the moment I named Nova and the significance that I found a way to encourage her that actually worked.

It wasn't just a tactic. It was the truth.

Nova is the brightest child I know. She's talented, wise, a big thinker, and intelligent. She really is a supernova, ready to shine brighter than anything in this world. It's my mission to constantly remind her of that and ensure she understands it for herself. The world can be cruel, but my job as Nova's mom is to shield her from the cruelness for as long as I can, while also teaching her how to combat it at the same time.

This is why the idea of bringing someone into both of our lives has taken a back burner in importance. I don't want to add anything else to our lives that would create discord, nor do I want to lose control over the normalcy we currently have. It's the sacrifice I choose to make for the sake of my Supa Nova's world, even if it means I put a pause on my pursuit of happiness in certain areas. I'll do it each and every time.

"**A**rms up."

Nina lifts her arms, and I run my fingers across the gown's beaded top. We are in an ocean-view hotel room, just outside the area of Lovey's Bay Beach, where Nina would be doing her bridal shoot. The air-conditioned room serves as our dressing room, a necessary accommodation before we step out into the heat that settles in early June.

Nina's dress for the photoshoot is a pearl-beaded bodice with a flowing tulle skirt purchased from Love x Lace. My stomach lurches every time I think about her using a perfectly good wedding dress for the shoot. Yes, she paid for it, but the gorgeous dress is likely to be a victim of an unintentional fire with her photoshoot plans. Nina's clumsiness makes this simple shoot a hazardous site. I send up a silent prayer.

Lord, please let Nina make it through this shoot as a beautiful bride and not a female Fire Marshall Bill.

"I can't wait to see the final photos. I just know this shoot is going to come out so well!" Nina says and then lets out a quick hoot as I tighten the criss-crossed ties running up the back of the bodice.

My lips tighten as I sigh, hopeful, "I'm sure it will. Have you and the photographer talked about how you'll accomplish the shot?"

Nina smooths her hands down the sides of the dress, answering confidently, "Yeah. She showed me a video she found on social media that showed how it should go. It seems fairly easy and harmless. Torch a small fireball in my hand and boom! Strike a pose!"

Nina animates her description with a high-pitched "boom" and wiggling spirit fingers.

In my head, everything that can go wrong flashes. Yet, when she turns to me, I force a smile and lace my response with shaky optimism.

"Yeah, that doesn't sound bad at all, girl."

Nina nods before heading over to a black high-seated chair, set up by her makeup artist. She begins to do minor touch-ups to Nina's eye makeup. "Yep, easy peasy. I wonder if Denzel and his crew are here yet…"

Nina continues talking a mile a minute while my

mind stays on the curiosity of whether the fire crew had arrived. Curiosity gets the better of me when I flick my gaze to the sliding door, only letting them glance over the boardwalk for a second. It isn't enough for me to see anything but the blur of palm trees. I roll my eyes and shake my head at my silly attempt.

This is so stupid. Just admit you want to see the man.

My body betrays me—heart pounding and breath held—just telling all of my business! A rolodex of images of Tevin scrolls through my mind, overwhelming with a rush of feelings. I want to see this man so bad, but I'd be damned if I let that desperation slip past my mind.

"Joni…"

Nina's chirp brings me back. She's standing in front of me with a beaming smile, oblivious to my mental antagonizing. Her forehead creases slightly as she asks, "I asked, are you ready?"

Was I? Not really. In a matter of moments, there's a high probability I'll be face-to-face with the man I hadn't seen in two months, who I used to call my…my…what did I call him?

My anguish causes the pulse in my neck to race, and I push out a cleansing breath. "Yeah. I'm ready. Let's get this show on the road!"

6

TEVIN

"...So this job should be a pretty easy one for your first job. Any questions?"

Denzel stands in front of not the shining cherry red engine we usually drive, but an old, retired engine dedicated to the Volunteer Squad. It's a dull tomato red, the color the fruit takes when it's about to rot. Just sad looking, especially against Denzel's crisp navy fire company collar shirt and pants.

I scan over the three volunteers for today, Kian, Maya, and Jace. They look left and right at each other before collectively shaking their heads. Denzel lifts a brow as he tilts his head to them. "Alright, well, if there's nothing for me, you're dismissed to get set up."

They waste no time dispersing. Of the volunteers left, I'm glad to have these three with me today. There's Kian, our quiet techy, who's somewhat hard to read. He always keeps a muted expression over his olive face, but never comes off as disrespectful.

Then, we have Maya Grant. She reminds me of Fallon a little, not letting the guys show her up, especially with drills. She's an open book, unlike Kian, letting us know her WNBA career with the number one women's team, the Damask Storm, was cut short last year due to an injury just before training season. Needless to say, she didn't heal fast enough and was eventually let go. That shit's fucked up, but she seems to be bouncing back okay, fully committing herself to rebuilding her life and her commitment with the squad.

Then, we know Jace. Just like at home, Jace carried a perfectionist energy with everything he did at the station. Even though technically he's a volunteer, he shows up with intentions to be more than just a volunteer. He's like the model student, always with questions and giving one hundred and ten percent at everything. I haven't told him, but Jace could be a good firefighter if he decides to take the path. Only time will tell, though.

"How do you feel about those three?" Denzel asks, taking a stance to my left.

I nod, answering confidently as I watch them collaborate in setting up the water hose and cones to block off the set. "For real, they are the stars of the squad. They'll do fine with this job or anything that may come up."

Denzel hums. "Good, sounds like their leader is doing a good job equipping them. They didn't even have questions for me."

Rotating my head to him, I twist my mouth. "Come on, man. This is light work. Just get the water pumping if we need it, and knowing Nina, we will."

Denzel chortles. "Yeah, we are talking about my Nina, but take it easy on my girl."

He slices me with a hard side eye, and I laugh, placing my palms up. "Just stating facts. No foul, my guy."

"Yeah, okay," he grumbles, lightheartedly. No more than two seconds later, he sighs, "You're right, though. I don't know why Nina insists on doing this kind of shoot, but anything for my fire-inducing girl."

"That's love!" I cackle, almost in perfect timing, as I catch Nina stepping out onto the boardwalk, dressed in a sparkling wedding dress. Denzel's energy is palpable and heavy as he goes pin-drop silent. I look to him and find him gawking ahead.

The sound of a girly laugh I'm all too familiar with has me scanning the entourage behind her. A jolt runs through my chest, and I stuff my hands into my pockets, trying to steady the anxious feeling taking over me from seeing Joni. She trails behind Nina, holding the train of her gown as they tiptoe across the boardwalk. She veers right, stepping off onto the sandy beach, putting them in direct alignment with Denzel and me. When Joni looks up, our eyes meet. That same ol' feeling takes over, where my heart buoys from my chest. I quickly divert my focus to…anything to keep from showing how happy I am to see her.

"I…I'm going to go check on the crew." I grumble, taking off in the direction of my crew. I didn't expect the jolt of energy running through me from seeing her. I thought that putting distance between us for two months would dull the pull she has on me, but it doesn't. Instead, her pull is even stronger, making it impossible for me to play it cool.

I'm down bad for her. Damn.

I felt like I was betraying myself with that thought, but I couldn't lie to myself. I had it bad for everything about Joni. Her laugh. Her smile. Her goofy ass and corny jokes. I love everything about her, which is why I'm messed up over being put in the fuck-buddy zone. Yeah, I know, that's what we do, but that's not all that we do, nor is it all that I classify us as.

"That's a new look for you, boss," Maya's voice gathers me together, and I turn to her, smirking and giving me a curious look. I furrow my brows, confused, before she tilts her head towards me and explains, "That smile. I've never seen that one before."

I try to act unaware. "Whatcha mean, Grant? This is the same smile I wear when y'all finally get shit right."

Maya doesn't find the same humor as I did in my shady shot at the crew and walks away as I hoped. Her clocking my sappy ass feelings is enough; I didn't need her figuring out who the culprit is. As she walks away, she throws over her shoulder, "You ain't talkin' about me. I'm the GOAT at everything I do!"

I huff a short laugh and shake my head, muttering, "Yeah, she definitely reminds me of Fallon."

After a few minutes of setup and test shots, the shoot is ready to go. I lean against the front of the engine, watching as an assistant trudges through the sand to Nina, carrying a spray bottle. I continue to watch curiously, waiting to find out the purpose of the bottle. I see someone else from the production crew move in closer to Nina, but not in the frame of the shot, with a bottle of Vaseline. I frown, still taking it all in, yet not making sense of any of it. Joni steps into frame to fluff Nina's dress before she and the photographer switch places. That's when the show begins. The photographer flicks the ignition of a long nozzle lighter just before the person with the Vaseline slaps a dollop into Nina's outstretched hand.

I suck in a cautionary breath just as I catch Joni's eyes on me. Her eyes widen, and my heart booms so loud it fills my ears. It happens. I get drawn into her gaze, and

I can't move my eyes away from it. Involuntarily, my face mimics the nervous smile taking over Joni's lips. Just as quickly as it happens, Joni blinks away, running her fingers across the edge of her short bang. Bashful Joni is another version of her I love, too. It's the only time I get to see her with her guard truly down.

"Get it together, Tev..." I scold myself, swiping my hand down my waves and over my face with hopes it would bring me back my focus. If that didn't regulate me, the commotion seconds later did.

"Oh, my God!"

"Watch out, Nina!"

JONI

I spotted Tevin the moment Nina and I stepped out onto the boardwalk. There was a big red firetruck, plain as day, at the photoshoot site, and several fire-fighters in their blues. It should've been hard for me to pick him out, but it wasn't. I know Tevin's frame with my eyes closed. I zeroed in on him immediately, standing beside Denzel.

"Aww, your man is here."

"Yeah."

Nina and I respond at the same time, her response audible and squeaky, while mine came out under a slow breath. Shocked by my words, I dart my eyes between Nina and the makeup artist. They're in their own worlds and missed my admittance.

Stupid...

Tevin wasn't my man.

Tevin can't be my man.

I pick up the train of Nina's gown as we proceed to cross the boardwalk. My mind is still mulling over my claim that no one heard but my consciousness. I shake my head, clearing away my intrusive thoughts and returning my focus to what's important right now: making sure Nina's shoot goes without a hitch.

Except, as Nina gets settled and receives her instructions, I can't help but steal a few glances at Tevin. God, that man is fine. He looks good in anything, but what gets my body going is when he's in anything fire-related. It's something about it that makes me want to set fire to my panties just for him to rip them off of me.

"Now, Joni..." I scold under my breath and then snicker at my lewd thought. But it is true. With him standing there against the fire truck, his chiseled chest creating soft lines under his collar shirt and his pants, slightly snug enough for me to imagine the temptation between his legs...I want him.

I'm so caught in my thoughts that I don't realize that he catches me looking at him. I tense and my eyes widen, then my nerves rattle when he smiles at me. I feel the heat collecting in my cheeks, and I can't risk blushing like a little ass schoolgirl. I dart my eyes down, brushing my hands through my hair for something to do besides ogle Tevin.

"Oh, my God!"

Hearing Nina's scream makes me whip my head in her direction, seeing the disaster unfold. The mound of lit Vaseline plops off her frantically shaking hand and onto her dress. In seconds, the flame combusts, trailing up the tulle of her dress. All I can imagine is Nina crisping into a fried Wedding Barbie.

"Watch out, Nina!" I shriek. I don't think twice before dashing over to her and swiping at the blaze.

It's like the flames are mad at me for jumping into the fight because the flame doubles and jumps on me, burning through my pants. I curse myself for wearing pants in this ninety-degree weather, but then my panic kicks in. I begin to flap my arms over the building flame, jerking back any time the heat scorches my hand, until— impact.

Grains fly into my face, and I pinch my eyes closed. Without sight, I can only hear the commotion: Nina yelping and Denzel's direction, and then the shuffling of the sand. There are other conflicting voices and sensory elements, but figuring those out is the last of my concerns. My leg was once up in flames, but now, I feel something rubbing on my lower extremities.

A body?

The weight on top of me and the heavy breathing clues me that there's definitely a human over me. The bulge colliding into my thigh has me fighting to push the man off me until I open my eyes to…

"Tevin!" I breathe, my heart pounding against my chest.

Tevin pins me with concerned eyes as he pants, "I got you. My pants…fire resistant…"

I look down along the length of us. His body cages me, his weight pressing me into the sand as the fire smolders out. My chest still heaves, but with more control as my gaze drifts back up his body, over his arms that clenched the side of mine, and then his honey-hued eyes —softer now, reminiscent of moments we shared before our fallout. God, I want to be back in that space with him. My eyes drop to his dark, perfectly pink-tinted lips, and I want them too, back in my space—on my lips. They are so close I can feel the warmth of his breath skate across my slightly parted lips. I blink my eyes back to his, hoping my thoughts aren't as transparent as I think.

"I thought it'd be a hot day in hell before you'd talk to me again." Without thinking, the words trickle from my mouth, followed by a short chuckle.

Tevin's eyes narrow, and I see the corners of his lips twitching, like he's trying to retain his smirk from turning into a full smile. My stomach hollows as the silence settles between us, until he mumbles, "Well, the temperature is dialed up to one hundred and hell degrees today."

I blew out through my mouth, my laughter colliding with his. All of a sudden, it feels like old times again, like it hadn't been months since we shared a laugh. My limbs fall limp underneath Tevin, and my head sinks deeper in the sand as the tension of the moments prior releases from my body. The only intensity left is the burn of Tevin's stare at me.

"You okay?" He asks, his voice low and serious.

"Yeah," cracks through the breath I exhale, feeling flushed by more than the beam of the high noon sun.

Tevin's eyes gleam with the same concern as before as he scans my eyes for truths unspoken. Fluttering my eyes away, I try to keep one unspoken truth to myself: I missed this man. My gaze lands on the cluster of people onlooking the scene, and quickly I remember we were in the middle of a photoshoot and Nina damn near set herself and me ablaze.

Squirming my way from underneath him, I half-heartedly joke, "You plan on lying on top of me all day?"

Tevin moves into a squat position before extending his hand for me, which I take, using his strength to help me from the sand. I begin brushing off the golden crystals from my top and then down my pants. When I stand erect, Tevin combs his fingers through my lightly bumped strands from the top of my hair down to my nape. I don't know if he meant to, but the pads of his fingers trace down my neck before he gently clasps his hand to the back of my neck. Reactively, I look up at him just as he takes his other hand and brushes the ends of my bangs to the left of my forehead. His eyes are shaded amber now and blazing with a look that always sent my center quivering and gushing for him. With a simple response, he reactivated the quiver and the gush of my center:

"Funny…you never had a problem with me staying on top of you all day."

"Mm-mm-mm. Today was a day."

I inhale deeply, taking in the scent of lavender sugar filling the bathroom. It lingers still in the steamy residue of my shower and is enhanced by the body cream I cup in my hand, ready to lather onto my skin. Lifting my right leg and propping on the side of the tub as I sit on the closed top of the toilet, I leisurely smooth the whipped butter onto my bare thigh, spilling from the flap of my satin robe. Massaging my own leg is no comparison to someone else's hands, but it does enough to relax me after a long day.

The photo shoot wasn't supposed to take half the day, but after the mishap with the fireball, we had to pause to make sure everyone was okay. Nina was fine, just a little frazzled and left with a gaping hole in her dress. We were thankful that the fire didn't turn into a breaking news segment for the six o'clock news, but we were left with no viable photos.

Nina balled at the news, rightfully so. I couldn't sit and watch my best friend's photo shoot be ruined. I offered her another dress from Love x Lace for her to borrow for the shoot, with a threat to her life if she ruins it. After two hours of switching her into a new dress and fixing her makeup, we were back to the beach and finally finished the shoot just before happy hour.

Nina wanted to celebrate and immediately called Fallon at the end of the shoot, but I wouldn't be participating in the happy hour celebration. All I wanted was to get home, take a long shower, and unwind. Any other time, I would be down to go to Rhythm and Brews and kick back, but after the day I had, being snuggled up at home was more appealing. What made it even more enticing is knowing that I had the apartment to myself, with Nova at her Dad's for the weekend.

Feeling lush after moisturizing my skin, I pad the short distance from my bathroom to my bedroom. The sunset fills the room with a burnt orange hue, casting shadows of the window blinds and the palm tree outside against the wall. I was in a lavender mood tonight, and the combination of a lavender and French vanilla scent, wafting from a flickering candle on my nightstand, added to the moody vibe, filling the room. I shimmy my shoulders as I tiptoe over to my made-up bed, giddy to slide under the comforter onto the percale sheets.

"Who would've thought this would be the highlight of my Saturday evening?" I murmur, not feeling an ounce of dissatisfaction while rubbing my feet together. I take a long sip from the glass of Prosecco I prepared before my shower, then awaken my phone to scroll through social media. After a few long swipes through pictures, my thumb pauses on one particular image. A smile ghosts over my lips as I read the caption:

LoveysBayFD: Nothing like a hot and fiery Saturday with the V-Squad!

My eyes skate up to the image again, landing on Tevin. He stands with the two male volunteers to his right, the one with the locs pulled to the back of his head standing beside him. The female volunteer stands to his left. He poses with his arms stretched over the shoulders of the man and woman, wearing a lazy smile. What catches my attention is how the female volunteer leans into him, nearly laying her head on his shoulder. I squint as I use my index finger and thumb to zoom in, searching for some sign of an untold story between them.

I sigh and let the picture go, realizing how ridiculous I am being over a simple picture of him with his team. If things hadn't changed between us, I would know the names of each of his volunteers and wouldn't be guessing the relationship between him and the gorgeous volunteer. I'm almost positive there's nothing between them, but not having him in the same capacity as I once did leaves room for my mind to speculate.

"I'm tripping," I mumble as I continue scrolling through my timeline. I have no business speculating over who Tevin may or may not be fucking.

"You never had a problem with me staying on top of you all day."

The echo of Tevin's words and then my thighs clench at the memory of how he held onto my neck, piercing me with those damn eyes of his, sends a chill up my spine. Tevin had a way with his eyes. Eye-fucking. He had a way of undressing and fucking you simply by looking at you with dark and lustful eyes. It made me hot every time, including our moment on the beach.

Ding!

I look up at the notification sliding from the top of my screen.

Tevin: Is you melted or is you thawed?

I snicker and bite on the inside of my lip at the unsuspecting text.

Me: Neither. I'm cool and cozy.

Tevin: That's interesting. You looked pretty hot out there earlier.

Is he flirting?

I lean back against the stack of pillows behind and pull my feet up, propping my arms against my thighs. Seconds go past while I scrutinize the words I want to respond with. Part of me said to take his words literal as fuck. It was hot as hell today, so I'm sure I looked like a roast chicken earlier. The other part of me believes he's flirting with me. It's what we did well—flirt and fuck. I detest the last part of my thought and respond neutrally.

Me: You did too.

The last thing I want to do is misunderstand and be on Love Island by myself. I stare at my screen intently, waiting for his response.

I hope he is flirting.

> Tevin: So we were just two hot and fine people on the beach today, huh?

Oh, he's flirting.

Chewing on the inside of my lip didn't halt the smile spreading wider on my face. It didn't stop the wetness that drew between my thighs. Nor did it stop my brain from overworking, trying to come up with something clever to say.

> Me: I mean, I don't know about you, but my face card never declines.

> Tevin: Oh shit, lol. Cast me out to the wolves then.

> Me: You know I'm joking. 😜 Your good looks never wear off... even if it's been months since I've seen you.

.   .   .

I can hear my heartbeat thudding in my ear as I watch the text bubbles dance on my screen and then stop. Instantly, I regret mentioning how long it's been since I've seen him, but I am curious as to what he will say. It seems like eternity passes when he finally responds.

> Tevin: Yeah, it's been a minute. I had to check on my favorite girl, though. You did almost roast before my eyes. 😂

> Me: Never a dull day with Nina! Lol. I'm good, though.

> Me: That's all you hit me up for?

It's dark in the room now, with only a slight amber hue being cast by the candle and the light from my phone. I know my last text is bold and a reach, but it's already sent. I run my fingers across the lapel draping over my right breast while holding the phone with my left, watching the bubbles dance again. Tevin doesn't have me waiting nearly as long as he did before.

Tevin: I may have missed you a little, too.

I purse my lips as I fight back my amusement at this conversation. My fingers tingle as they get busy typing my response.

Me: I've missed you, too.

I stiffen at the bloop of my text sending and immediately begin to fret.

What am I doing?

Getting what I want.

At least I hope so after throwing all caution to the wind and confessing my longing for him. No playing it hard to get. No making him wonder. Just straight up confessing. Although it's a simple confession, my body's prickling, my nipples hardening, and my pussy throbbing all tell my truths. I miss him and I want him.

Does he want me too?

Tevin: Wyd?

Me: Nothing. Just got out of the shower.

Tevin: 😌

Tevin: Probably smelling all good in that lavender body cream you like.

A giggle escapes me, realizing he still remembers my favorite scent. I don't know what I thought; it's not like years passed, just a couple of months. A couple of months too long. Sinking deeper into my pillows, I cross my right leg over my left, letting the flap of my robe fall, exposing my moisturized thigh. I wiggle my toes as I respond.

Me: I smell good, but maybe I chose a different scent?

Tevin: Yeah, right. You love that scent as much as I do.

Me: Lol! I could have. I like change every now and then.

Tevin: Yeah, right! Just like I know you probably still chose that little ass robe to put on. You probably got those glistening ass thighs out, too. Am I right?

Tevin: Cat caught your tongue? 😆

The cat caught more than my tongue. My legs clench tightly, trying to contain the spill of my juices, but with my mind running wild with thoughts of the miracles he performs with his tongue, there's no holding back.

Me: No, just relaxing a little more.

Me: But you're right.

Me: Lavender sugar and a robe covering my body. Except my thighs.

I know I'm playing with fire. Did I care? Absolutely not. With Prosecco in my veins, my brain is floating with the wave of my arousal.

Tevin: Relaxing, eh? You must be alone.

Me: I am.

Ask him, my brain encourages, but my thumbs shake as they hover over the screen, fearing rejection. Another woozy wave of Prosecco runs through my veins, and I throw caution to the wind.

Me: Come over.

Tevin: Want some company?

Me: The door will be unlocked.

8

TEVIN

It isn't Joni's snoring that stirs me awake this morning. Her snoring is surprisingly soft. It's her snuggling further into my chest and the slight grip she has on my waist as she continues to sleep that pulls me awake. The memory of the night before becomes clearer with each blink.

The sun beams through the window behind us, crisp like an early sunrise. I figure it can't be more than six in the morning, partly because of this, and also because my body doesn't like sleeping past that hour. For a few moments, I indulge in her display of affection, cocooning her in my arms as I stare up at the rotating ceiling fan, but an indifference begins to settle.

So, about last night. I had a few beers. Rhythm and Brews bottles a house-brewed IPA, and Jace and I stopped by to grab a case after wrapping up the workday. Besides Nina's snafu, everything went without a hitch.

Was I buzzed when I texted Joni last night? Yeah, but I was in my right mind and knew reaching out to her could go very right or very wrong. I couldn't get her off my mind after we left the beach. Feeling her in my arms again felt right, even if it was because I was saving her from being lit the fuck up.

My intentions were pure at first. It was all shits and giggles, like old times. But the jokes slid into flirting, and then the flirting had me tossing Frenchie a good night and driving across town. You know the rest. We were back at it as if we had never stopped.

Now, here I am, rejuvenated, pussy drunk, and conflicted. I want to stay here, listening to the quiet hum of her breathing, but I know I shouldn't. Even after an amazing night, the memory of our encounter before still lingers in my mind, and I didn't want to risk being thrown out like Jazz from The Fresh Prince. I had to leave with some dignity and my heart intact this time.

I ease myself out of bed, inching myself from underneath Joni. I don't realize how close to the edge of the bed I am until I thud against the carpet. Joni pops up at the sound, leaning over the edge of the bed, peering at me, confused.

"Damn, my bad," she apologizes, thinking she is at

fault. She tosses her hand down for me to grab as she quirks a smile that pulls my heartstrings.

I plop my back onto the floor and lie there trying to figure out how I will make my exit without second-guessing myself. There isn't an easy way to do it, so I push out a breath and then slowly bring myself up on my side to fish out my boxers from the pile of clothes. Without looking at her, I say, "Nah, that was all me. I was trying to get out of bed without waking you. I gotta head out."

"It's early…" she says, her words holding a slight disappointment and then trailing into a giggle.

I'm standing now, pulling my boxer briefs over my hips. I let out a deep sigh, my chest heavy yet strong as I choose my dignity over giving in again. Standing on business, I shift my morning wood and then lean down to swipe my T-shirt from the ground before turning to her, saying, "Nah, I'ma head out. I don't want to be thrown out like my name is Jazz again."

I didn't plan for the last part to come, but fuck it. That's how I felt.

"Really, Tevin?" Joni's brows knit as she sits up sharply, clutching the sheet over her chest.

I slowly bob my head up and down, pulling the shirt over my head. I have to turn away from her puppy-dog eyes because I can feel my reconsideration tugging at my brain. I can't tell her I want to be here just as much as she wants me to be, or does she? There's a part of me that doesn't want her to just want me here for a short time, because I want to be with her for a long time.

With my shirt on, I pad towards the bedroom door, where I found my sweats and step into them, choosing to say nothing. I could hear Joni shuffling through the sheets and then her light footsteps against the carpet, following me out.

"Tevin…Tevin!" I hear her call out. Her voice goes from a soft plea to an irritated whisper. I stop in the middle of the living room floor, letting Joni round me. She stands before me in her robe, her eyes big with disbelief. I didn't want to hurt her, but setting this boundary will. I can't help but operate with softness in mind with her. I place my hands on the sides of her arms, rubbing up and down before I lean down, pressing my lips to her forehead. I hear her softly exhale when my lips touch her skin. I pull back, returning my gaze to hers.

"It's all love, Lil' Bit," I breathe. The corner of her eyes softens, furthering her disappointment. I inhale sharply, gritting at the same disappointment. "I'll see you… Okay?"

I didn't know whether the next time I'd see her would be sooner or later. I had to figure some shit out, and she did too. Last night reinforced how much I saw her as more than just a friend with benefits. She is a friend I want to make my lady one day, but she won't let me into her life beyond the surface.

Joni's mouth parts slightly, like she wants to say something. Fearing the uncertainty of her words, I kiss her firmly. She tenses to my aggression, then melts into me, her mouth softening against mine. The flicker of her tongue against mine makes me lightheaded, and I palm the back of her head for steadiness and to push my tongue deeper into her mouth. I savor her taste before I reluctantly break the kiss, moving my hands to cup her face, planting one more kiss on her lips. She flutters her wanting eyes up to mine.

"I'll hit you later, alright?"

It's a rhetorical statement, but I wait for the few seconds it takes for Joni to nod her head before I drop my hands and slip into my slides, sitting at the front door. With a pat to my sweats, I hear the jingle of my keys. I will myself not to look back, leaving my heart with the woman who doesn't know she owns it.

"So we want you to enjoy the summer, but remember these three things if there's a fire emergency: Get out or away from the fire and stay away from it, know where your meeting spot is outside of the danger, and…can you guys tell me what the last reminder?"

I lift an eyebrow, surveying the classroom filled with primary colors and black and brown second graders. One kid stands up, an outspoken and energetic boy who'd been the standout of the class. I tilt my head towards him to answer.

"Y'all are our homies!" He quips, his toothy smile beaming.

"Yeah, kid," I respond, chuckling along with the crew standing beside me. I notice the young teacher grimacing and shaking her head. "You're right. We are your friends. So, if we are on the scene, don't be afraid of us. Listen to our instructions. We want you to be safe. Got it?"

A collaborative "yeah" rolls through the classroom before the teacher takes over, asking the students to thank us for our time and instructing them to work on the crossword puzzle and coloring activity that accompanied the reason for our visit to Sunny Bay Elementary School.

It's our annual visit to highlight our campaign "Fun in the Sun Safety," teaching the kids how to stay safe and fireproof during the summer. We always schedule in June, right before summer break. With holidays and fun ahead, it's a great time to educate kids on how to stay safe—and their parents, too. It's also a good way to make the kids familiar with us and know that we are always there to help keep them safe. The volunteer squad usually spearheads this campaign, which is why I am here, leading the way with Maya and Jace.

"Mister…" The teacher says, her voice drifting as she moved her eyes down to my chest. Her eyes squint slightly, seeming to read the name printed on my shirt over my heart before they soften and meet mine again, confidently completing her sentence. "Mr. Clarke."

Her smile is soft and warm, just as the way my name lilts from her. I quirk a half smile, correcting, "Yes, but you can call me Tevin."

"Okay then, Tevin." She giggles. The same smile

simper as she grazes her bottom lip over her glossy lips. "Would you and your crew mind staying, just a little while longer, while the students work on the last activity?"

She peers up at me with round hazel eyes, reflecting her question and hope as she tucks a bouncy brown curl behind her ear. The slip reveals her face a bit more: red-blushed cheeks that set off her tawny skin, pink, plump lips, and those eyes. Between those eyes, her sweet voice, and the further protrusion of her lips, I can't tell whether she's asking for herself or the kids.

I clear my throat, moving my eyes over her head and over to the class. Jace and Maya were wading between the tables around the class, interacting with the students. I return my gaze to her still steady one.

"Sure, I don't see why not, Mrs...."

She places a manicured finger up, halting me. "It's Miss. Miss Bradner, but you can call me Shelby."

She uncurls the rest of her red-painted fingers, holding her hand out towards me. Naturally, I take her hand for a handshake. She strokes the inside of my palm with her thumb. My eyes widen, then relax, catching her flirtation. She arches a brow and smirks before purring, "Thank you," and sauntering away, my eyes moving like a pendulum to her sway.

That's new, being hit on by a school teacher—a fine school teacher at that.

I chuckle at my surprise and redirect my focus to the class, my curiosity landing on a little girl situated on the outskirts of the class. What pulls me to her is that she is rocking pink headphones over her curly pigtails and sporting glasses that match the color of her headphones. Then it's the way she puckers her lips in frustration and then slides the page with the crossword puzzle to the end of her desk, pulling the other sheet in view and grabbing a crayon. When I made it to her desk, her dark brown eyes lit up, slightly startled.

"Hey, kid, mind if I sit with you?" I ask, widening my smile, hoping it would erase the shock from her face. It did, her eyes softening as she pulls her head-phones down and lets them hang around her neck as she nods.

I pull up one of the chairs from a nearby table and sit beside her, squatting down on the chair that's suitable for only elementary-sized kids. With my knee nearly in my chest, I try to get comfortable in the hard chair, relaxing my arms on them. The girl continues to fill in the fire hat outlined on the sheet in front of her. I glance over at the sheet she abandoned, a crossword puzzle with five puzzles and clues. I can tell she tried one of the puzzles, as evidenced by the light color of the lead still present from what she tried to erase.

"This question seems a little hard," I say, pulling the crossword puzzle in front of me. I point to the puzzle she previously worked on and then read the clue, "Opposite of 'cool'…for letters. Hmm…cake?"

"Her giggle catches me off guard. It was loud and chattery and oddly reminiscent of one I feel like I've heard before. She looks up at me with big brown eyes that seem familiar, too. "Cake?! That's food!"

I chuckle at her amusement. "Yeah, you're right. Maybe that's my stomach talking. What's your guess?"

Her smile weakens, and she returns her attention to the paper, shrugging. I slide the sheet closer to her. I see her glance at it before she brings her focus back to coloring.

"It's hard for me," she mumbles, picking up another color and starting to color in the turnout gear.

"It's a little hard for me, too. That's why I wanted to see if a superstar like you could help me figure it out. You know, teamwork?"

She slowly twists her head and looks up at me. The way her eyes widened slightly, I could tell I piqued her interest. "My mommy calls me superstar."

Got her. I muse to myself, feeling like I am one step closer to the goal. "Ah, I'm spot on. Well, what do ya say, superstar? Help a guy out?"

Her little reluctant smile settles in the left corner of her mouth. "I guess."

"Cool."

I exchange her coloring page for the crossword, flipping it over and aligning it with the edge of the box we're solving. It blocks out the rest of the crossword puzzles, leaving only the box, the clue, and three words, one of which includes the correct answer.

"Okay, so now that we know it's not 'cake'…" I nudge her shoulder, making her giggle again. "Let's see what our options are. The opposite of cool is…hot?"

I grab the nearby pencil and begin writing the letter H and then O before she places her little cinnamon hand over mine. She moves her head from side to side, "No, that's incorrect. 'Hot' is only three letters."

"Ahh, right," I say, playing along and erasing the letters. "See, this is why I need your help. You're keeping me on my toes."

When I glance over, I see that her smile has lifted. Timidly, she slides her pointer finger over the paper and points to the correct word, guessing, "I think it's heat."

"Oh, that's a good one! How about you write your guess in?" I flick the eraser end in her direction. For a moment, she looks at it hesitantly before moving her worried pupils to mine. I nod my head to her, encouraging her to try. With a quiet sigh, she takes the pencil and begins to fill in the box. When the word fits, her smile beamed like the sun's rays. I put my hand up for a high-five. "See, I knew you could do it, Superstar."

She slaps my hand, letting that giggle loose again.

She corrects, "My mommy is the only one who calls me Superstar."

I laugh, shaking my head. "Okay, so what should I call you then?"

She points to the name tag on her desk.

My chest jumps as she answers, "Nova…Nova Skye."

JONI

"Your server will be here in just a few moments, but while you wait, Chef Maxwell would like to send his regards by way of a complimentary bottle of our best."

As scoring a table on Sable Pearl's new rooftop dining on Friday night with no reservation isn't enough, a polished waiter arrives with a shiny wine glacette, cradling a wine bottle. An incohesive "Ooh" rolls over our table and then cheers as the sound of the forceful corkscrew pop floats through the warm, salty air. It's the perfect yet unsuspecting start to our girls' night, overlooking the calm waters of Lovey's Baby as the sun starts its journey to set for the night.

"Now, tell me again, why aren't you giving Maxwell all of your time?" Fallon leans onto her elbows, balancing her wine glass between her fingers. She pings her with narrow eyes and an arched eyebrow, full of curiosity that also filled me on why she wasn't bagging the owner of Sable Pearl.

Zaria leans back into her chair, sipping her already perspiring glass of white wine slowly. Her lush hair is pulled up into a messy, sultry bun with tendrils framing her face. The white tube dress shows off her toned shoulders and arms. She sips slowly from her already perspiring glass of white wine before catching the remnants of her sip with her tongue. "C'mon, Fallon. I've been here all of three months, and I have so much to concern myself with than settling down with a man already. Can I get to know my new city? Get further into my studies?"

I sip from my glass and grunt my disapproval before saying, "Girl, you better snatch up your man before someone breezes in and snatch him up for you. Chef Maxwell is the literal catch of the day for the single and mature demographics."

"She is right," Whitney murmurs into her cup as she peers above the rim at Zaria, who feigns ignorance of our warning with a light chuckle.

"If things are meant, it will be a thing. Right now, I'm focused on me and getting adapted to my new life here in Lovey's Bay, since I have to do it on my own now that my bestie spontaneously jumped the broom. Couldn't even wait for me to come back into town."

All eyes shoot to Fallon, whose jaw has now dropped at the conversation bouncing to her. She sits up straight, fumbling with the thin strap of her satin burnt orange dress, obviously looking for her words. The light breeze tussles her grown-out brown and blonde-highlighted bob, forcing her to tuck the piece falling over her eye behind her ear as she scoffs, then laughs, "Oh, that was so dirty of you. Taking the spotlight off of you playing hard to get and putting it on me."

Zaria shrugs smugly and poses, "Well, tell me I'm lying about it."

"We all know she ain't lying," I chime in, cackling. "You're lucky any of us made it to your impromptu wedding, girl!"

Whitney puts a hand up. "Wait, fill me in. Fallon, you came and bought that dress from Love x Lace and got married soon after?"

"Soon after?!" I quip. "How about that afternoon, Whit. She couldn't wait to marry ol' Big Head Deacon."

Whitney gasps while Zaria laughs at my dig. Fallon twists her mouth into a sheepish smirk as she sips from her wine. "You damn right. Big Daddy and I had to tie that knot *real* quick."

I gagged. "Oh my God. Please refrain from calling him Big Daddy at this table."

"Big Daddy, Big Daddy, Big Dadddddyyyyy," Fallon sings, gyrating her hips in the seat, making the table break out into laughter while I fake being sick.

Our server came over to quickly interrupt us to grab our appetizer and meal orders before we continued to cackle and muse over Fallon's story about her wedding day and the events thereafter. Immediately after their nuptials, Fallon and Denzel hopped a plane to an exclusive island resort for her brother's wedding. It wasn't just any wedding; it was the wedding of the decade. Her brother was marrying the infamous Tinsley McCoy, and it was the talk of every pop culture blog for many reasons. There were conversations about her being stalked, but no one knew the identity of the person.

Additionally, there was drama surrounding her ex's feelings about her moving on. And then, there were rumors of some commotion happening during the week of the wedding. Fallon confirmed this was all true without giving away the juicy details we all wanted.

"We still can't talk about everything that happened," Fallon admits, after pouring herself another glass of wine from the second complimentary bottle we received. "But what I can say is, some of the rumblings in the blogs are true. It was a mess before it was beautiful. Hell, Deacon and I were on the job while out there!"

"Nuh uh! Not working and not getting paid!" I exclaim, scrunching my nose up.

"Where they do that at?" We all turn to Whitney, who is wholly invested in the story, and start laughing. Not so bashfully, Whitney shrugs her shoulders and giggles, "I'm just saying."

"Girl, if you aren't a little Joni," Fallon says, shaking her head.

I cackle. "Ha! No. That girl is a little Jasmine Guy. Look at her and tell me she doesn't look like she spit her out."

Whitney groans and raises her hand. "Joni, don't start the shit. We aren't going over this again. I do not look like that woman."

"Like hell you don't! And you are just as prissy as Whitley."

The table grows silent for a beat while Zaria and Fallon dissect Whitney with their eyes like she is a science project. Whitney wouldn't be able to get away from the comparison, especially not now. She's still dressed in her work outfit, a sleeveless linen black dress with turtle-shell buttons down the middle. Like almost every day, her hair is in bouncy curls, cascading over her shoulders.

Zaria tilts her head. "Well, if I'm honest, you do look like--"

Whitney's gasp is amplified and long. "Not you too, Zaria."

The whole table falls out again.

· · ·

There was so much to catch up on between us. Well, mainly Fallon, Zaria, and me, with Whitney just being all ears as the newbie to our crew. We were missing our glue, Nina, but tonight she and Denzel were cake tasting. Their nuptials were scheduled for the end of the summer, and time was ticking to finalize all the wedding details.

Zaria shared about her transition from the fire to the medical field, while Fallon caught us up on married life as we enjoyed our dinner and then more wine. Every time we finish a bottle, a new one would come out, complimentary. We were on our third bottle, and the sky was now a deep navy when my head started to feel light-headed and my eyes heavy with the effects of the libation. When I became slightly aroused by the short buzz from my phone on my thigh, I knew maybe I needed to slow down.

Tevin: Whatcha getting into tonight?

Maybe I didn't need to slow down just yet.

Me: Out with the girls.

Tevin: Hit me when you're done?

"Who got you cheesin' over there?"

I flutter my eyes up to Zaria's sing-song voice. She's looking at me with a glint of curiosity in her eyes and curiosity playing against her pursed lips.

"Tevin."

"Avery."

"Oop! Now that's tea!"

Flabbergasted, I dart my eyes from Fallon to Whitney and then to Zaria, who is pinching her thumb and index fingers together repeatedly. All of them gleamed sheepishly at me.

"Y'all heaux always yappin'," I mumble between pinched lips as I point to both Fallon and Whitney.

Fallon throws her hand at me. "Girl, everybody knows you and Tevin fuckin'. Hell, y'all may be fuckin' more than me and Deacon...well...maybe not..."

I scoff hard while mentally admitting that Tevin and I did have a time and lots of sex, before things hit the fan recently. "Not! I don't think anyone can keep up with you and Deacon's fresh asses!"

Fallon shrugs and smirks smugly as she turns her glass up, gulping down the last of her wine.

"Joni might be telling the truth. I haven't seen Tevin around much lately, but Avery…well, he's been sending her flowers and stopping by for lunch for the last two weeks."

As soon as Whitney spills it, Fallon and Zaria catch all the "tea", gushing over the gossip.

"Wait, who is this Avery?" Fallon asks. "Let me find out you are finally taking my advice and building your roster."

I snicker and bring my nearly empty glass to my mouth, thinking about the night Fallon and I went to the speed dating event, when she gifted me her verbal handbook for bagging the men. Before Deacon locked her down, Fallon had every fine man knocking at her door, making her handbook certified. I never took on her advice, though, being content with the casual thing Tevin and I were doing.

"Not really. We haven't really been hanging out like we used to," I admit, placing my glass onto the table. I sigh drowsily, lining the rim of my glass with my gel manicure. "Y'all know Nova keeps me busy. I don't have time to be juggling men."

Fallon's eyebrow piques. "School is out and summer is in. It's time for Mama to have some fun. But, back to Avery. Who is this guy?"

Instead of waiting for me to respond, which I didn't plan to, she turns to Whitney expectantly.

"He's the brother of one of the clients from Love x Lace. He came in with his sister, and while she eyed wedding dresses, he eyed Joni. And…he's a looker himself. Tall, chiseled jawline, silky wavy hair…and paid."

"Ooo, we like paid," Zaria chimes in, wagging her finger in the air.

"Damn, girl, were you looking or nah?" I screech, turning my lip up at Whitney.

She sucks her teeth. "You were taking too long to give them the details. Just like you're fittna take too long and miss out on a good sexy summer with your excuse being Nova."

"She has a point," Fallon adds under her breath.

My jaw slacks slightly as I look between Whitney and Fallon incredulously. "It's not an excuse. It's a very factual reason why I have not dated *at all*. I come with a lot—a lot meaning, a whole kid that I don't want to confuse with multiple men coming in and out of our lives."

"I get it," Zaria says, slumping into her seat a little deeper and crossing her legs. "My best friend when I was a kid, her mom used to introduce us to a new 'uncle.' Uncle Kenny, Uncle Paul, Uncle Charlie…you know, the funny thing is, Uncle Charlie's last name was Wilson."

The sound of the distant waves crashing was all that was heard for a few beats as we all stared at Zaria with indifference before breaking out into laughter.

"Z, shut your drunk as up!" Fallon cackles before getting semi-serious with me. "I hear you, Joni, but just because you're a Mama…mamacita…doesn't mean you can't have a little fun."

"Yep," Whitney chimes in. "What did Jody's mama say in Baby Boy? Mama gotta have a life too? You need one too. If anything, it will give Nova an example of healthy love…when you do meet someone. But you gotta get out there to meet someone."

My phone buzzes again, and as I look down at the lit screen, I assume it's Tevin texting me again.

> Avery: The Moon's beam is almost as beautiful as your smile. Wishing on the few stars out tonight for you to finally accept my date. Have a good night, gorgeous.

I nibble on the inside of my lip, trying to contain the growing smile and the bursting fireworks in my chest. Before I can dim the screen, Whitney leans into me, taking a peek. She snatches my phone and turns it to Fallon and Zaria.

"See, this man wants her…bad! He's been asking to take her out every chance he can get."

My phone gets passed around the table while I sit there, stuck like Medusa has stoned me.

"Girl, and he's smooth with it," Fallon coos as she reads the text. She moves her eyes to me and lifts a brow. "Joni, don't become an old spinster, still using Nova as an excuse not to date, and she's good and grown. Shit, don't use her as an excuse now. Like Whit said, use her as motivation to show her that there's love to be found. Shit, if anything, get your back blown out a few good times while Nova's gone for the summer. She's leaving in a couple of weeks, right?"

I almost forgot I told them about Nova spending July with her father after her two-week summer camp for the rest of this month. At this point, the crew knew my schedule and prospects, and they were holding my heels to the flames, trying to burn away my resistance to letting loose a little. It wouldn't hurt for me to take Avery up on the date…or get my back blown out by Tevin…or someone knew all together. The point is, I had time and plenty of opportunity to kickstart my dating life again, whichever way I chose to go, while Nova would be away.

I look down at the white linen covering the table, dragging my words, "Ya'll might be right."

"Oh, we are right! Which is why I accepted the date for you." I jerk my head to Whitney, who is typing away on my phone. "He's already hearted the message."

"Jasmine Faux-Guy!"

I rip the phone from her grasp as the table laughs at my expense. I look down at the text thread, seeing that Avery, in fact, heart the message Whitney sent and then read his suggestion for our date. My fake annoyance fades as I roll my eyes up at my group of friends, low-key excited for what's to come. Maybe Mama does need to have a little fun.

"Deac the Freak!"

Heads swivel in my direction as I call out to Deacon. His back is turned away from me, and I only know it's him from the white Lovey's Bay Fire Department logo on the black of his navy T-shirt—oh, and his square noggin. He slowly turns his head, revealing a twisted scowl with a hint of a smirk.

"Tiny Tev! That's what the ladies call you, right?"

I slow my steps before expelling an exaggerated, "Haa!" and then, "You stay clockin' my shit, my guy."

Deacon daps me up as I approach, retorting, "Says the one walking through the bar calling me Deac the Freak?!"

I shrug and continue laughing, not really having

anything to say back to his observation. There are two barstools open on either side of him. I take the one on the right, but pause before sitting, turning to the guest I had forgotten was accompanying me for a second. "Yo, D, I don't think you've met Jace yet. Jace, this is Deacon. Captain over at Company 143."

Deacon swivels completely around and steps down from his stool, pulling Jace into a dap-hug. "Jace… Carter, right? Your reputation precedes you, my guy."

I nod my head to Jace in agreement as I sit down. He pulls back from the dap with a hesitant smile. "Oh yeah?"

I suck my teeth at his lack of confidence. "I told you, man. You're killing it and need to stop playing about and go through the Fire Academy."

Jace sits down while Deacon leans back onto the bar, looking at him with amusement. "You're thinking about the Academy, eh?"

He huffs a short laugh as he runs his hand over his locs. "Something like that…"

Jace has been doing more than thinking about it. He's been ruminating and obsessively indecisive over it, and I didn't get it. Well, I did kind of. Jace is still hung up on his past and holding himself hostage by it with his thoughts, but the kid is good. He's always head down when it comes to learning the protocols that come with being a volunteer firefighter and asking questions about life as a professional firefighter. I can tell he wants to do it, but he's his own hang-up.

"That's a good look. We need more young guys like you," Deacon encourages. He swivels around on his stool, catching a bartender passing to place another round. "What's your hang-up?"

"His jailhouse blues," I answer for him. Jace deadpans at me, and I continue, looking between him and Deacon. "I told him nobody was worrying about that but him. He wouldn't be on the V-squad if that were the case."

"It's just the V-squad," Jace speaks up. "You know it's hard for felons to get a job out here. I know y'all helped a nigga out with the volunteer stuff, but—"

"No buts," Deacon chimes in. "We don't do favors. We bring on talented and dedicated individuals, especially those in the volunteer squad. Lift your head, bro. Sign up for the Fire Academy."

The bartender came back with a round of shots—brown liquor. Deacon slid one my way and one to Jace. "Cheers, my guys."

I bring my glass up, meeting Deacon and Jace's before taking it to the head. I hiss, long and intensely, as the poignant liquor burned down my throat and chest. Deacon lets out a satisfied "Ahh," and Jace grimaces quietly. Regaining my composure, I grunt, "What are we cheering to?"

Deacon shrugs lazily. "Shit, I don't know. To life. Committing to our decisions."

I slap Deacon on the back. "Ahh, shit. You regret married life already?"

Deacon balls up his face, twisting his head to me. "Hell, no. I got the best thing since sliced bread."

I raise my hands in surrender. "My bad, my boy. You sounded a little regretful."

"Shit, no regrets at all. I'm happy to be off these single roads. I'll leave y'all to man that." Deacon looks over to Jace. "Besides a major increase in pay from what you're getting with the Squad, you'll get an influx of ladies as a firefighter, too. Tevin will tell you."

I bounce the topic back to Deacon. "Shit, you and Denzel can tell that story. Y'all are the ones with major commitments."

"Fill me in," Jace inserts, a curious grin spreading across his face. "The ladies really be checking for us?"

Deacon guffawed. "Tuh? Do they? Denzel met his fiancée while working a call to her house."

The thought of walking into Nina's apartment, smoky and oven damn near scorched, only to find out it was some broccolini that caused the fire had me cracking up. I held my stomach as I added, "Yes, our guy fell in love with the most notorious firestarter we've ever met. We should've got the cops involved and slapped her with arson."

The two of them laugh with me before Jace speaks up. "Damn, and I here I was thinking Tevin getting play at the Elementary School was just a stroke of luck."

"Oh, it was a stroke of luck!" Deacon howls.

"Aye, not too much on me, my guy," I say, cutting my eye at him. "You know I get play. Stop frontin'."

Deacon places his hands up in front of him. "Okay, okay. You do. There's Joni, Miss Mouth All Mighty." He breaks out into laughter again, and I nudge him with my elbow. When he settles, he returns to Jace's comment. "You pulling chics at the volunteer gig? What's Joni gonna say about that?"

"Joni *can't* say anything," I correct, leaning my elbows against the bar. I go into a slight daze as I stare at the liquor bottles before me. "We're just friends."*I've been friend-zoned.* "I didn't follow through, though. I was on the job, and it was somewhat blurry whether she was flirting or just being nice, ya know?"

"Well, looks like you have your chance to see whether she was flirting or just being nice. Look who's walking up."

I look at Jace, who nods his head in the direction, looking past me. Before I could look to my right, the sweet almond and musk scent I remember distinctly from the visit to the elementary school wafts to my nostrils, followed by the beautiful one who wore it, sliding into a barstool beside me.

"Miss Shelby." The words drop from my lips before my brain can catch up.

Placing her clutch in front of her, she smirks and bats her flirty eyes. "Just Shelby will do."

"Thank God for summer breaks!"

Shelby's words come out almost like a moan, dragging slightly over her alto, hinting at her inebriation. I wouldn't say she's drunk, but she's a little lit from the fancy martini she ordered. At the end of her words, a flirty laugh breaks out as she drops her head back. Her curls sway with each swing of her head. I grip her small waist, cautious of her balance as her back continues to bend backward.

Without warning, Shelby whips her upper half up, pressing her chest into mine. She pins me with sultry eyes as her exposed thigh snaps to my thigh, her flowy skirt of her dress bunching at the apex of her sheened, toned thigh. Reactively, the pads of my fingers sink into the thigh—again, as a precaution. We were on the dance floor, and the last thing I wanted was for her to tumble in the middle of all these people. That's what my brain repeats, but my dick jumps at the arousal of it all.

Shelby, more aware than I thought, giggles before she does some ballroom-style twist, steadies herself on both feet, and grinds her backside into my groin, running her fingers down my neck as she dances.

Miss Shelby. Miss Shelby. Miss Shelby.

I stopped referring to her by that when she asked hours ago, but in my head, that's what keeps rolling through. She gives Ms. Parker from the movie Friday vibes. You know, on the outside, she looks sweet and innocent with her bouncy curls, batting gorgeous, hazel eyes. But, behind those eyes glimmers something that says, when no one is around, she's not so innocent. Her dance moves, the way she presses her hips into me, and the way her words float with seduction laced—it all screams sexy, teacher temptress you want to get to know.

Joni.

I shake my head like a snowglobe, willing the thought of Joni out of this moment, but like the last hundred times she crossed my mind, the thought of her stays put. Each time, guilt pits my stomach and fills my woozy mind. I can't pinpoint why. Is it the mix of the beer and shots I scoffed down with the guys that brought out my mixed feelings? Or is it because I know that Joni and Shelby know each other through Nova? My stomach lurches at the thought of how messy it looks, but—

We're friends.

Her words exactly.

With that, there's no real harm in me enjoying the end of my night with Shelby. Jace moved on a while ago, conversing with Shelby's friend, whom I think is named Whitney. And Deacon, my only walking reminder of Joni, left about an hour ago.

"Oof, I need a little fresh air. It is hot in here," Shelby groans when the music switches to something slower. She fans herself with her hand and asks with her eyes before verbalizing, "Walk with me outside?"

"Of course."

Shelby slips her fingers between mine and begins leading me towards the exit. Looking over my shoulder, I locate Jace, lifting a finger, hoping the gesture tells him I'd be back. I catch a nod from him before I focus on the sway of Shelby's hips.

Shelby Bradner is model-esque, from body to face card, but I wouldn't be doing her real justice if I didn't say her personality added to her allure. Conversation flowed effortlessly between us. She's light-hearted and playful, not missing a moment to hit the dance floor and dance her heart out. I like her energy and how it made my heart race. She's like your first ride in a sports car, because she's sexy and fun, you feel sexy and fun. I felt like…I was enough.

"Thank you for escorting me out."

Shelby releases a sigh as she fans herself again. I can still hear the muffled song playing inside Rhythm and Brews as we stood on the sidewalk outside the building. There's light foot traffic on the street, which is not unusual for the time of night. I look down at my watch, confirming it's nearing midnight. The soft tap of her heels on the pavement encourages my eyes to look up, finding her sauntering over to the brick wall of the building, where she falls limp against it. She tosses her head to the side, flashing a tempting smirk.

She doesn't have to ask. I amble over to her. As I stop in front of her, she moves her head so that she's looking up at me. The street light illuminates her angelic face, slightly covered by the large curls. I swipe a few curls from her gaze. She slowly blinks her eyes at me, tasting her bottom lip. Chortling, I ask, "You okay?"

"Perfect," she says in a near whisper. "Tonight was so fun. I didn't expect to run into you again."

"Ha," I chuckle. "Me neither, but I can't say that I'm disappointed."

She stands up straight, but is still slightly shorter than I am. She lifts her head to level our gazes. I can feel the heat permeating from her body, and my nerves tingle at the reaction. After a beat of us scanning each other's eyes in silence, she proposes, "We should do this again… soon."

Hell, yeah, is the thought that immediately plays in my mind, but I opt out of verbalizing it that way. "We should…next Saturday? I have a busy week with the fire duties, but I can make some time Saturday, if you can."

Shelby steps closer, her pebbled nipples brushing

against my chest, and trails her fingers down the side of my face. "I'm all yours Saturday."

In my head, I see it happening, but I didn't expect it actually to happen. Shelby leans in and presses her soft lips to mine, sealing her confirmation of our date with a kiss.

"Don't touch that handle."

Avery places his massive hand over mine, pausing me from shifting on the cool leather seat of his BMW. I hadn't planned on touching anything in this car. While we travelled, Avery ran down the specs of the luxury car. He told me it was a seven-series and a model toy for a "tech geek like himself." His words. I didn't question him. It had all the trinkets you could ask for, including touchscreen displays throughout the driver's console and door handles, as well as warming and cooling seats. I found that out because I accidentally hit a button, initiating my seat to warm up. I didn't realize it until my ass felt like I went to the lower room on a fire chariot. Besides not wanting to ignite anything else by accident, the car just felt like I should sit pretty with my hands in my lap. Shit, it smelled expensive, scented like a new car mixed with leather and spice. It smells just like him in here, too, expensive, leathery, and spicy.

Don't get me wrong. I've been around nice things and affluent people. That's all I'm ever around for, for the most part, at Lace x Love. But Avery is wealthy. He's a senior-level executive for a tech company, and on top of that, he comes from a long line of old money. I recall his sister, Davina, discussing how her wedding would be held at Bayview Country Club in The Coves, a land of opulence. It's where old, long money lived, and all I needed to know was that he had money I'd never seen before. I'm a girl from the northside of the city limits of Lovey's Bay and have never stepped foot in The Coves in all my life, so it's safe to say that the type of wealth and lifestyle he's used to, I'm not. We hadn't even started our date, and already I was nervous and felt out of place, even though Avery hadn't done anything to make me feel this way.

The soft click of the door unlatching pulls me back into the moment, and as it lurches open, I send a silent prayer up that when I get out of this car, there isn't a puddle of sweat and an imprint of my ass on the tan leather.

"I have to tell you again. You…look…amazing."

Avery steps back and admires me as I stand. Immediately after stepping outside of the car, I can feel the sticky humidity from the earlier rain plastering to my skin, but that wasn't it. I can feel Avery's admiring gaze roaming up my body, from my newly pedicured toes in the strappy heels to my freshly shaved legs, and then rounding the curve of my hips that peeked through the thigh-length flowing summer dress I chose for today. It's a simple, white dress with soft floral imprints, plunging seductively at the neckline. When his smoldering eyes met mine, he blew out a quiet breath, making my cheeks heat.

"Stop it, Avery," I gush, accepting his hand. He moves his head from side to side, still adoring me with his eyes. "But then again, keep doing what you're doing."

I giggle as he brings the backside of my hand up to his mouth, pressing his lips to it. "Oh, I can go on for days, but then we'll miss this movie."

"And that we are not doing. I heard *Bloodline* is good."

The jitters that play in my nerves are traded for my eagerness for the movie. We decided to see *Bloodline*, the new black thriller by rising director Roxy Creed. Having been in theaters for only 48 hours, it's already receiving rave reviews, and even I, typically not the gory thriller kind of girl, am excited to see it. Roxy Creed isn't just a black female director; she's killing it in the movie business.

"Same," Avery agrees, clasping his palm into mine. "They are saying it may be Roxy Creed's best film yet. Can you believe they are saying that about her first thriller?"

"Hell, yeah, I do!" I boast, immediately stiffening at my uncouthness. Avery's charmed smile juts my apprehension away, but I proceed to shift my demeanor. "Roxy is talented beyond her time. She could write a silent movie, and it would be top tier."

"Touche." Avery gently moves me to his left side, placing him nearest the street. He confirms the crosswalk is clear of traffic before he slips his arm around my waist, leading me towards the Black Tie Theatre. He looks down at me. "Well, guess we'll be the judge tonight, eh? I'll lend you my shoulder in case you need a hiding place from all the vampiric gore."

Avery winks his right eye, softening my reserve even more. I twist my mouth at him. "Let me introduce myself to you again. I am Joni "No Scare" Morrison. I'm a G in these scary movie streets!" Avery throws his head back, his baritone carrying through the air as he cackles. " I ain't scared of no vampire!"

13

TEVIN

"**I** love vampires!"

"What?" My question emerges through a chuckle that I hope conveys my amusement. The way Shelby shifts in the plush leather theatre seat so that she can look at me suggests she understands.

She nods quickly. "Yes, vampires. Vampire movies, books…you ever heard of viggas?"

"Ha!" I guffaw, shifting slightly so I can look into her doe eyes.

I'd be remiss not to take another glance at her. She's a knockout, just like the last time I saw her. Tonight, her hair is tousled into a high ponytail, accentuating her beautiful, lightly made-up face. She wears a satin shorts romper that hugs every curve of her body. The way she sits in the chair pushes her breasts together, making it hard not to notice her pebbled nipples or the dew that sheens her brown thigh. I blink my eyes to hers, redirecting my focus. "What are viggas?"

"Vampires who are like us…you know…"

"Viggasssss…" I drawl as the name begins to make sense, cracking up. "Okay. I dig that. Where'd you come up with that?"

"I didn't come up with it," she emphasized, pointing at herself before letting her pink tips trail between her cleavage. "It's a term I picked up on in some of my reading. There's this romance author named Christina C. Jones and she wrote a series about black vampires. She called them 'viggas.' It's probably where my fascination for vampires expanded past my teenage love for Twilight."

"So you've been about that vampire life for a minute, eh?"

Shelby touches her lips as she snickers. "I guess. I know, it sounds weird—"

"Nah." I reach for the hand that traces her lips, prompting her gaze to smolder. I chuckle, "It's interesting. I just didn't know black women like vampires and shit."

"Oh, we do," she purrs, weaving her fingers into mine. "Especially those of us who read her work. She describes them in a way that I know they are fine. And, it's something about the mystery of them and how they use their fangs as a sexual enhancement..."

Shelby trails her tongue across the ridges of her teeth as her eyes hood. Fuck, everything she does is so sexy. I clear my throat and stretch my neck, attempting to work out the kink—all pun intended. The waitress returning with our mondo-sized popcorn, a Sangria for Shelby, and a beer for me was a welcome distraction.

Shelby's sex appeal is a problem, and I can't tell whether it's good or bad for me. I'm not used to a woman coming on so strong and so fast. This is only our first date! Don't get me wrong, we shared a few back-and-forth texts before tonight, and it was a vibe. Like I said before, she has a dope personality. Tonight, however, having her in front of me, giving me these hypnotizing eyes and hella sexual energy, I can't tell if she's for the streets or she has the hots for me.

I wonder what Joni's doing...

There it goes again, the parlay of Joni into my mind again. You'd think that after not hearing from her at the end of her girls' night last weekend, I would've learned to let her occupy less of my mind. I didn't. I fail every time when it comes to Joni. All I think about is her if I let my thoughts run rampant—like now, instead of on my date.

As the movie about black vampires in the early 1930s unfolds, Shelby proves not to be as brave as she claimed when the gore begins. She's startled and yelps at every jumpscare and buries her face in the pit of my arm every time blood splatters. However, when the few sex scenes cross the screen, her prowess comes out, snuggling closer, and I even felt her trailing fingers move past my arm to the top of my thigh at one point. When she travels a little too north, I shift and politely move her hand.

Who am I, and where did my game go?!

Turning down advances isn't like me. There's no question I'm attracted to Shelby, but something… someone…

I just didn't want to take it there with her.

Shaking my head, I return my focus to the scene playing, where something seems off with one of the humans, and they are going around eating garlic to prove they're human.

"If you smell something, I just shat myself."

The random commentary in the middle of the very serious scene obliterated the silence of the theatre. Everyone, including myself, breaks into laughter, with one obnoxiously tittering laugh catching my attention. For a hot second, I think it could belong to Joni.

I roll my eyes up, annoyed with the lack of control I have over my thoughts.

Under my breath, I scold my betraying mind, "Get… a… grip."

JONI

et a grip, Joni.

As soon as my "Little Engine that Could" laugh, as Tevin once called it, leaves my mouth, my hand flew up to it. I hoped it would be stifled by the onset of laughter in the theatre from the comical line from the actor in the movie, but when I shifted my eyes to Avery, he was looking at me.

"That was cute," he chuckles and then takes my hand, reassuringly.

The breath I unintentionally hold breaks free from my chest, and I relax back into my seat. I let him squeeze my hand and then caress the top with his thumb, further soothing away my embarrassment.

Every moment I want to be embarrassed at myself, Avery peeps it and subtly affirms it's nothing to be embarrassed about. At this point, I'm realizing that the only person it's bothering is me, but I didn't understand why. I've never felt so nervous and uneasy around anyone—any man. Well, the only man I'd been around before Avery is Tevin, but the fact remains that I never felt like this. Tevin has seen and heard every quirky sound or tidbit that makes up me, from my laugh to my obnoxious snoring, yet I never clammed up or thought twice about it.

And here I am, thinking about Tevin again while on this amazing date with Avery. This all started when Avery and I were walking into Black Tie Theatre, and I saw someone who resembled him. I only saw the back of the person, but I knew Tevin's front and back very well, or so I thought. I remembered scanning the theatre lobby, trying to identify the person I saw outside, but I had no luck. The lobby was crowded with people, and Avery swiftly whisked me through it to our theatre, all while my mind reminded me that I didn't respond to Tevin's text last week.

By the time the girls and I left Sable Pearl, I was like two sheets to the wind. We were all dizzy in our inebriation, and when my rideshare dropped me off at home, I passed out. After that, the weekend and then the week were a blur with work and getting Nova to and from summer camp. The thought of Tevin didn't occur until now, and that was unusual in itself.

Tevin and I have been weird with each other for a while, and the way he left the night after Nina's fire mishap solidified it. It's been hot and cold, more on the cold side between us, with neither of us stepping fully into how we used to be.

How we used to joke.

How we used to talk.

It's why I went on to accept the date with Avery, even after Whitney committed to me. Tevin and I had just been different... even though, technically, we are just friends, and the way we are now is technically how we should be as friends.

Yet, here I am, running down the reasons why the state of Tevin and my relationship is okay, despite my chest swelling with uncertainty.

"You okay?"

My vision adjusts to the scrolling credits before me, realizing I missed the closing scene. I twist my head towards Avery.

"Yeah, I'm good. I-I was thinking about that ending," I lie.

Avery bobs his head up and down, agreeing, "It was profound for sure. You need a moment?"

Surprised that my excuse made sense to him, I shake my head and proceed to pull up from the chair.

Avery assists me to stand, and we begin our shuffle through our row. There's no point in rushing. We attended a sold-out showing, and the whole theatre was slowly yet productively dispersing. A cool blast of air hits me as we reach the aisle, sending immediate relief through my body. Still holding my hand, Avery continues to lead with each step down towards the exit.

As we round the corner that leads to the door, I stiffen in my steps, my eyes meeting Tevin's glare. It's for sure a glare, even under the soft lighting of the short hallway. It burns through me, causing my veins to tingle, but then, when my eyes expand on the whole picture, taking in the woman hanging onto his arm, my body grows cold, and the gravity of my heart plummets.

"Pardon us," Avery says to Tevin and his date before gliding in front of them, still with a comfortable grip on my hand. When we are a few steps closer to the exit, I look over my shoulder, catching a glimpse of Tevin through the sea of people between us. It's a quick, blurry glimpse, but what's clear between the two of us is the myriad of questions we silently mirrored.

15

TEVIN

Did I really see…?

Yes.

I know every inch of Joni from her petite frame to her beautiful face.

That was her gorgeous face.

And her petite frame in a dress I've never seen.

…With some cornball ass dude.

"That's funny. I think I just saw one of my students' parents. I can never get away from my little love bugs," Shelby says with a giggle, reminding me that she is clinging to my arm. Suddenly, her cleave to me gives me the icks, and I step to the side, creating some space between us. She looks stunned by my shift. "Uh…is everything okay?"

I didn't want to come off as a prick, but my thoughts

were running rampant, all of them running to one destination: Joni.

Who the fuck is this guy?

I inhale slowly, trying to remain in my date and not crash out over the fact that Joni is on one, too.

"Yeah..it's just…it's not stuffy in here to you?" I breathe out, feeling my forehead perspiring. Her fallen smile returns softly as she shrugs indifferently and continues before me.

With Shelby in front of me, it gives me the solitude to scan the crowd of people for Joni, but that shit was like trying to find a needle in a haystack. The lobby is packed with the crowd for the late-night shows as well as those filing out of theatres. I scan the crowd. No Joni. No S-Curl wearing square either.

Since when did she date squares, and how did she meet this one?

I feel defeat thudding against my chest when I reach the exit, and still no sighting of Joni.

Shit hits a little different when you see the holder of your heart on the arms of someone who's not you.

"The night is still young, don't you think?"

Shelby poses the question as we step out into the muggy night air. It smells like rain, and I can tell it rained while we were inside from how thick the air is with humidity. There's a distant lightning bolt crawling through the sky that indicates maybe another round is approaching.

I look one more time for Joni. When I stretch my gaze over the parking lot, I spot her getting into a sleek, luxury ride. A lump clogs my throat.

"Tevin?"

Why does she keep calling me?

Shelby's voice was no longer tantalizing to me. In the moment, she sound like an annoying ass bird, chirping my ear and I grimace as I roll my eyes to her. Her eyes pop, obviously taken aback by my expression. Pinching my eyes closed, I breathe in, deep and slow, reminding myself that Shelby doesn't know the turmoil going on inside of me. When I open my eyes, I pull out my phone and tap on an app.

I breathe, "Shelby, I had a great time, but I just realized I left something unhandled...something important..."

Joni.

That's the only person flashing in my mind.

She is what's important to me.

I left our situation unaddressed, essentially cracking the door for someone to slip in.

I gave up on scrambling for a solid reason to give Shelby when I look back and see an empty parking space where the luxury car once sat. That's when my blood pressure spikes, and thankfully, it's also when my phone chimes the confirmation I was waiting for.

I look to Shelby, my brow lifting slightly apologetically as the rideshare I requested pulls up.

"I'm sorry. I really have to go, but I've arranged for a car to take you home. It's on me, but please, let me know when you make it in."

The disappointment is palpable on Shelby's face—beet-red cheeks, and her jaw nearly hits the pavement. Still, I try to stay a gentleman, pulling her into a side hug before opening the door of the Black SUV for her, but as soon as I slam the door closed, I bolt to my Jeep with one destination in mind.

The silence during the fifteen-minute drive to my apartment was thick as the air, a telling sign that rain is on the way. Saliva pools in my mouth from my mind being fixated on Tevin and Nova's teacher taking precedent over the simple act of swallowing.

How the hell did he meet Ms. Shelby?

The question looms over my head like the dark cloud creeping over the yellow moon tonight. The parallel of the inner and outer world feels ominous, and my fingers tremble against my lap. I'm not scared. I'm reeling with emotions that I can't pinpoint, because it all boils down to this: Tevin and I aren't together.

He can go out with whomever he wants.

I can go out with whomever I want as well.

So why am I fuming and feeling possessive over the

fact that I am not the one he chose to go out with tonight?

Avery lets out a chuckle that brings me out of my thoughts.

"What's so funny?"

"Nothing. I was just thinking about that one scene in *Bloodline*…"

Avery proceeds to describe the scene, and my mind veers off again. I didn't care about the scene. The only scene I seem to care about right now is the intrusive picture developing in my head of what Tevin and Miss Shelby could be doing right now. I feel my fist balling as the picture turns lewd.

Shelby is gorgeous, and that's what has my stomach in knots when I think of them together. They looked good together. Hell, they're probably closer in age, and she probably doesn't have the hang-ups I have about acting on how I feel about Tevin. Shoot, the way she hung off of him, I'm sure she is fully open to him—in every way.

Ugh, what am I doing? I internally scold.

I hate this.

I roll my eyes and drop my head onto the headrest, stifling back a groan.

I don't realize we are in front of my apartment building until I hear Avery pulling on my door to open.

"Thank you for a great night," I say, stepping out of the car.

My voice cracks as my thoughts still travel to my ideations of Tevin and Shelby. Avery tries to hold on to my hand, but I quickly slip it away and blink away from his confused wince. I didn't have the energy to explain. I didn't want to. The only man I wanted to touch me right now is Tevin.

With a weak smile, I offer him a lie, "I'll talk with you…later?"

Avery drags out an "Okay…" before he ambles back to his side of the car and glides off.

I hope that his lack of words or attempt at a good night kiss means he understands this is our first and last date.

It's dark now, even darker than moments ago, now that the storm clouds have rolled in and covered the moon. Only the tall street lamp gives light as I walk the sidewalk to enter the outer corridor of my apartment complex. To the left and right of me are hallways lined with apartments. I trudge ahead and down the almost pitch-black hallway that leads to the elevator and a stairwell ahead of me, which in turn leads to several floors of apartments and eventually the rooftop.

The light that usually gives off a soft glow in the hall is out, per usual, and I'm ultimately relying on muscle memory to lead me to the elevator. When I hear footsteps behind me, my mind stops sulking and becomes alert.

Blame it on the jumpscares from Bloodline.

Blame my spiraling brain.

I bolt ahead.

With each clack of my heels, I hear another pair of shoes behind me, and I keep running, eventually passing the elevator and directly to the stairwell entrance.

The logic behind it? I had none. I was more spooked than I expected after seeing *Bloodline*, and now the only reason I could think of that someone is chasing after me is because they want my blood. If it's some vampire cosplaying as a human, I have a better chance of losing him by activating the strength of my legs from my years of running track. I grab the door handle and twist, letting the door swing open as I zip through it, praying that my heels or my flapping dress wouldn't make me the stereotype of every thriller movie that includes a black person.

I want to laugh at myself for the illogical explanation for this, but when I hear that the door doesn't click behind me but hits the wall and the steps quicken, my breath gets caught in my chest, and my legs start moving at rapid speed. The walls become a blur as I take on each flight.

The first floor.

The second floor…and then the third.

My chest burns with each pull of air as I hit the third

floor, but it didn't stop me. I can hear the footsteps still close behind me, and as I round the corner to the final floor, I take a glance, only making out a masculine figure behind me.

"Shit, shit, shit..." I whimper as I shift my gaze back ahead, locking into the door on the final floor. From taking this flight of stairs before, I know the door I'm pushing through would lead me to the rooftop—a dead end. I skid to a stop and turn to face my demise.

"Tevin?!"

"What the fuck you running for?"

Tevin throws his hands up to his side, looking incredulously. His chest is heaving just as heavily as mine. I palm my forehead, swinging it from side to side in disbelief, but then drop my hand and tilt my head at him. Eyebrows buried between my eyes, I answer him with a burning question:

"Why are you chasing behind me like you're out for my blood?!"

"Your...what?" Tevin breaks from his perturbed expression and belts out in laughter, keeling over and placing his hands on his knees. Nervously, I laugh, still wanting an answer, but laugh. Instead of answering me, he poses another question. "So, it was you at the movies with that greasy, S-curl-wearing square?"

I want to laugh, but I won't give him the pleasure of my humor, because...the audacity to question me?

I fold my arms and scoff, "A square, Tevin? At least my date looks like he has a brain. As far as yours…."

I knew it was a low blow, but whatever.

"She's a teacher. Very smart, actually. But, the way ol boy forehead was greased from the curl activator, I probably could've shined that bad boy up and been able to read his thoughts if he had any."

"Ha!" I tighten my lips, stifling my laugh. Tevin's screwed mouth twitches at the corner as if he wants to laugh, and I had to turn away from him to regain my composure. I walk to the brick wall enclosing the rooftop before I turn on my heels to him and quip, "You're jealous."

He scoffs now. "I am not jealous of that cornball."

He takes a few steps towards me, and I continue, putting up a finger for each point I make. "The name-calling. The questions. You following me back to my apartment…"

"You called Shelby dumb," he points out, stopping inches from me. He folds his arms and lifts an eyebrow as if he had checkmated.

I fold my arms too.

"The word 'dumb' never came out of my mouth. And I know Shelby very well. She's Nova's teacher." I tilt my head to the side, knowing I indeed played the winning move. Tevin opens his mouth and then closes it as if he is re-thinking his response. I take his silence as a moment for me to reiterate, "You're jealous."

There's a light above us that beams over Tevin, revealing the moment his eyes darken. He still says nothing, leaving only the crash of the waves on the bay and a distant rumble of thunder in the background. The woosh of the air conditioning system starting and the steamy condensation smoke billowing from it towards us startles us both. Tevin keeps his eyes on me as he finally responds.

"Jealous of what? You're mine. You've always been mine."

The tremor in his voice sends a shiver through my body, finding resonance in my center, and my knees threatened to fail beneath me. I slowly blink, and if I waited a second longer to open my eyes, I would've missed the ghost of a smirk in the corner of his mouth.

"Whatever, Tevin," I say, the words cracking as another rumble of thunder cracks through the air.

"Am I lying?" He unfolds his arms and steps closer to me, my nipples brushing against the material of his shirt. My nerves are firing off as he places his thumb on my bottom lip.

"I don't know what you're talking about," I muster to breathe, denying him the truth he seeks. I twist my head away from him, ungluing from his intense gaze. With my subtle movement, I can feel his fingerprint swiping against my lip before he cuffs the back of my neck with his hand. Mentally, I curse myself for the way my body melts to his touch.

"Am I?" Tevin challenges, his tenor breathy and full of lust now.

My brain is screaming, "No," but my ego won't let me win.

Or is it from the breath he steals as he massages the back of my neck with his thumb and trails his fingertips between my thighs and up my dress?

I don't move, and there isn't enough oxygen flowing to my brain for me to think. I feel. I feel his fingertips grazing my center against my damp panties. I run my tongue against my bottom lip as I feel him move the fabric to the side and circle his fingers in my wetness. His touch sucks out a shaky breath from my parted lips, and then a broken moan falls as he circles my swollen bulb.

"Feels like you're mine," he murmurs. He flicks his thumb, causing my body to spasm at the sensitivity, then presses two fingers into my center. I'm so slick that they sink into me with ease. My breath breaks through forcefully through a quiet moan. I pinch my eyes closed, still refusing to answer. He hums as he strokes his fingers in and out, "Mm-hmm, definitely feels like you're mine. Are you, Joni?"

He plunges his fingers deep inside of me and stills. My breath stills at the top of my inhale, and my eyes flutter open to his, piercing me with dark desire. And then, he curls his fingers inside me, physically motioning for my answer to come forth while massaging the spot only he has ever discovered to break my flood gates. I felt my essence spilling from me as light misty rain pelted my chest, yet the one word he wants to beckon stays lodged in my throat.

A heavier drop falls on my upper lip, and I feel it trail down to my bottom. Tevin leans down, taking his thick tongue against the droplet. It dissolves somewhere in between his saliva and my lip as he slides his tongue across the fullness of my bottom lip before sealing it with a smooch.

He doesn't stop moving his fingers, but only changes his pace from beckoning my answer to thrusting his way for an answer. In and out with firm strokes that had my knees weak and my right leg climbing his leg. Eyes still locked and our breaths nearly in sync, Tevin bends his knees just enough to lift me and thrust his fingers back into me. I'm gagged, only with another energy to whimper my pleasure and wrap my legs around him tightly. With my back against the wall and his arm around my waist to keep me from scraping against the rigid brick, Tevin continues to pound into my leaking center with his fingers.

"Don't play with me, Joni," he grunts, his eyes burning into mine. "Say it."

I'm panting now, legs shaking, body quivering, alerting me that my climax is near.

"Say it."

"Yes, Tevin…it's…yours…!"

And then my levy broke.

The fireworks went off.

My climax echoes through the air as the sky breaks loose.

JONI

The remnants of sleep weigh heavily on my eyelids as they flutter open halfway and then close again. The soft warmth that came with the sun's beam through the vertical blinds above my bed, and then the coolness of the sheets wrapped around my hips, created a contrast that gave me comfort. Then there was Tevin's arm wrapped around my waist, his warm hand palming my breast from behind, making me never want not to be his little spoon. The low hum of the central air whirring throughout the apartment almost lulled me back to sleep, until a rush of cool air brushes against my bare upper half as Tevin shifts. I shift with him, turning onto my other side. He's lying on his back now, stretching his arms above his head, his muscles pulling and contracting over his bare chest before he begins to peel himself up from the pillow.

I reach for his arm as he props himself up with his elbow, his lower half still dressed in the sheet. He looks over his shoulder with soft, drowsy eyes. I imagine my eyes show my hesitation to voice what I want from him. My eyes twitch from wide to steady as my heart pounds in my throat, until my voice cracks, "Stay. You…you don't have to go."

The words rush out desperately as my being fell back into the memory of the last time he was here. The bed hadn't even warmed before he got dressed and left. It was the first time I felt like…a booty call. After sitting in my feelings, I realize perhaps that's what he felt when I placed him in the "just fuckin' zone." In any form, I didn't want to feel that way again, nor did I want him to think that's how I saw him.

"I can't…" Tevin starts, his baritone heavy with sleep. When his eyes met mine, my lip protruded slightly into a pout. I didn't plan the intrusion on my face. It took up residence when my heart dropped with his denial. Tevin's mouth stays parted mid-sentence before he closes into a smirk and slumps back against the pillow. "…I can't stay too long. I got a shift starting at the station this morning."

The thrum against my chest slows with his explanation and his settling on his back beside me. He proffers his arm as my pillow, and I accept, sliding under his armpit and then gliding my leg up his hairy thigh. We lay there in silence, my fingers trailing down the middle of his chest as it slowly rises and falls. His fingers massage the tapered hair, now curly from the rain of last night, on the back of my head. His touch has a drowsy effect on my body, slowing my breath and sending tingling sensations everywhere.

"What are we doing, Joni?"

"I mean, I'm down for some morning dick if you down to give it to me."

"Ha!" Tevin hoots. He catches my nose between his pointer and middle fingers, and I squirm to get my nose from his grasp. "Be for real, Lil' Bit."

I snicker, giddy to hear my nickname coming from him again. "I am being for real. Last time you left me without a morning salute."

Tevin chuckles, but not nearly as hard as he did moments ago. It fades slowly, indicating he is in his thoughts. I'm in my thoughts too, because I knew what he was asking from the beginning.

"You know...I don't think of you as just a fuck, right?" My words come out slow and low, quivering with each syllable.

I feel him shrug underneath me. "Yeah. You made it clear. I'm not just a fuck but also just a friend."

I scoff and tilt my head up to him. Over his stubble

chin, I can see the straight line his lips are making as he looks up at the slow-rotating ceiling fan.

"Tevin."

"Joni."

He's relentless, with his words and the stoicism written over his face. He said nothing more, letting the silence circle us back to his initial question. I sigh as I shift my head to look at the door to my closet, chewing the inside of my lip as I ponder what to say, how to say it, how much to say. Tevin beats me to the punch, speaking first.

"I can't watch you going out with another man. That shit fucked me up, just as much as hearing you refer to me as somebody you just fuckin'. We fuck, but you can't tell me you don't feel something more when I'm deep inside you."

My center pulse and my walls clench instinctively at the thought. A tinge of pain is felt as my teeth clamp down on the small piece of my lip I'm still chewing on, an attempt to hold back the quiver that threatens to take over my body. The way my flesh reacts to the phantom feeling of him inside of me betrays any lie I may want to give about the feelings I feel for Tevin.

I no longer try to disguise it.

"I do."

A beat passes before I feel his chest vibrate as he asks, "So why do I feel like I'm the only one being vulnerable? I've been an open book since this thing started, and I still feel like I only know half of you."

I sit up onto my hip, taking a portion of the sheet to my chest. My offense displays in the scrunch of my face before it comes out with my words. "Tevin, don't do that. I've never kept anything from you."

Tevin moves his eyes to me, eyebrows lifted. "Nothing? So the part of your life that includes Nova is nothing?" My mouth hangs open, stalled from being able to rebut. His brows relax as he places his hands behind his head and continues, "It's like I'm good enough to know the inside of you, but not all of you."

A breath falls from my throat, my mouth still hanging open. Feeling my lips dry, I close them, settling into the silence that came with Tevin's truth. It wasn't my truth, though. I don't think Tevin isn't good enough to know the most precious part of me, Nova.

"She's the most precious part of me," I admit through the shallowness of my voice. I swallow back the lump that tries to settle in my throat. Water threatens to fill my waterline as I think of my baby girl. "I hold her close because I don't want to see her break…if I break."

Another beat of silence settles between us, and it deepens as the AC system clicks off. I'm looking down at the sheet, my pointer finger of my free hand zigzagging down the sheet mindlessly. I hear Tevin shift before I feel his arm around my shoulder, pulling me into his chest. I lay there with my ear against his chest, listening to the drum of his heart when he speaks.

"You're like my Gina to my Martin. My Pam to my Tommy. My Big Shirley to my Cole—"

"Big Shirley?!"

I whip my head up to see Tevin laughing into his hand. I sit up, never mind the sheet falling to my waist, and fold my arms. His laughter falls into a snicker as he undoes my folded arms and pulls me into him. I straddle him and rest on his chest, my chin supported by my folded arms. "All I'm saying is, you're my good thing, and with all good things, you treat them right. All I want is the chance to really show you I'm more than this big dick…" He pushes his semi-hard piece against the slick of my folds. He pulls me up to meet his lips. "…a chance to show you and your little one I'm the real deal."

I scan Tevin's eyes for a breath, seeking any uncertainty. When I find none, I wrap my arms around his neck and peck his lips. He slips his tongue between the sliver of my lips and seals his certainty with a deepened kiss. For the first time in weeks, it feels like things are alright with Tevin and me. No hazy lines. No blurred, smoky lines. Just us, mirroring our truths about one another.

· · ·

Tevin stayed about two more hours before he really had to go. No, he bolted, realizing that he overslept the 15 minutes he allotted himself after giving me the morning session he left me without after our last encounter. Fifteen minutes turned into an hour, leaving him roughly an hour to get back across town to his home, shower, and then drive another 15 minutes to the fire station. This time, I had no room to pout; I needed my man to keep his hard-earned job.

My man.

Look at me, claiming Tevin and shit. Truth be told, he's always been mine in my mind, but my heart wouldn't crack open enough to let him in. After yesterday, seeing him on a date with a gorgeous woman, then him not ending the night with her but with me, followed by the bare, no skeletons conversation…there was no way for my heart's door to stay jammed. If that wasn't enough, Tevin knocking all the Mario coins out of my hot box last night and this morning is the bonus that flung the door wide open. Tevin was mine, and no Shelby girl would prosper.

"I'll text you later," were the last four words out of Tevin's mouth as he stood between the half-opened front door of my apartment before he planted a kiss on my forehead and then my lips. His back met my acknowledgement as I watched him jog off in his undershirt and slacks from last night. His button-up flapped in his arm as his hard bottoms pelted against the cemented ground.

"Fun night, I see."

Unaware of anyone in the hallway, I tighten the lapel of my satin robe, moving my eyes to meet the voice. It was Zaria. She's leaning against the door of her apartment—Fallon's old apartment—with her arms folded and a curious smirk. She's dressed in scrubs, cluing me in that she must've just come in or is leaving for her hands-on instruction. Either way, there's no telling how long she'd been standing there.

I roll my tongue over my teeth, trying to compose my grin as I say, "Mind your business."

She chuckles as she turns to open her door. I begin to slip back into my apartment when I hear her call, "We'll talk later!"

"Later" didn't come for the rest of the day, which is fine with me. All I wanted to do was bask in the light beaming over me after having some normalcy between Tevin and me again as I did my Sunday cleaning. I almost didn't want to shower off the memory and residue of him, but I love my hygiene more, and I did before cleaning my apartment from room to room. By the time I received the text from Nova's dad that they were pulling up, it was close to five in the afternoon, alerting me that my Sunday and weekend were nearly over. I took the ten-minute heads up to plop down on my couch, letting the lemon, lavender, and bleach scent swirling in the air bring me added satisfaction. My phone buzzes against the glass table in front of me, and I grab it, smiling immediately.

Tevin: What are you doing?

Me: Waiting on Nova. She's about to be here. Shouldn't you be out fighting some fires or something?

Tevin: Don't speak that ill over my day. 😂 It's quiet today and I like that. Besides, I was involved in a major fire of desire last night. 🖤 I need a break.

I throw my hand to my mouth as I cackle and snort at the message.

Me: Let me find out if you're about to be an old man before I'm an old woman.

Tevin: Shit. I'm already an old man. You keep me young. 😬

. . .

Rolling my eyes, I grin, thinking about what I want to respond next. The rap of knuckles on my door pulled me out of my thoughts.

Me: Nova's here. I'll text you in a bit.

My phone chimes before I can set it back on the table.

Tevin: Tell her I said hi.

I know Tevin is testing to see if our conversation was just fluff or real movement toward something deeper. If he didn't know already, I'm already deep in this with him, but what he's confident about is the fact that I still had a leg hanging out on the shallow side. If I really wanted to see what could be of us, I had to allow him to show it, and that opportunity comes with introducing him to Nova, at some point, somehow. I don't respond; instead, I place the phone on the table and head to the door.

"Mommy, I'm hoomme!" Nova sings as I open the door. In the same movement, she threw her little body on me, wrapping her arm around my waist.

"Hey, Superstar," I sing-song back. I bend down so that I can plant a kiss on top of her frizzy ponytail. The ponytail was loose with baby hair frizzing across her edges. It was nothing I didn't expect after being with her father all weekend. "Go put your stuff away, boops."

Obediently, Nova takes off around me and to the right, down the hallway to her room, leaving me and her father.

"Malik."

"What up, Joni?"

Malik Banks tucks his hands into his relaxed-fit jean pockets as he nods to me. The white T-shirt he wears is a similar fit, relaxed yet fitting enough to show off his stocky physique. Fully clothed, you'd think he's stocky in a teddy bear kind of way because of his 5'9 height. I knew, however, from the time we were together that it was all muscle under there, thanks to years of high school and college football. In the past, that dimple, that smirk, his body, and how he then and now keeps a fresh lineup and 360 waves, would've had my insides melting. Now, nothing happens, except the tightening of my lips as an awkward silence settles between the two of us.

There was no bad blood between the two of us, even though part of the reason we are not together is that he was a real human dog, sniffing after every tail that wagged. If I am candid, I stayed with him two years too long, mainly because we have a child together. I knew we weren't equally yoked, but like many of us women, I stayed in the relationship because we had Nova, until that reason wasn't enough and proved to be unhealthy. When I finally woke up, I left with my respect and desire to give Nova a better picture, a picture of her two parents loving and co-parenting her—separately.

"So, I'll be picking up Nova after her field trip on Friday, right?" Malik asks.

Tired of holding the door open with my hand, I lean against it and fold my arms. "Yep. I already told the camp she'll have her little suitcase when I drop her off."

"Cool, cool. What about her hair, because you know I—"

I snort. "I know you know nothing about hair. She's getting her hair braided on Wednesday, so all you have to do for the month is make sure she wears her bonnet at night."

Malik's eyes balloon. "What about swimming?"

"She's good to swim with her braids. Just rinse her hair really good when you get out of the pool."

His expression softens as he nods and exhales away the hint of worry. "Cool, so I guess we're straight then."

I shrug, coolly. "Yep."

"Aight, well, I'll see Nova Friday."

I give Malik a little wave as he tilts his head to me before swaggering away.

It takes a couple of hours for Nova and me to get settled. Nova hopped into a bubble bath while I prepared a quick dinner, baked chicken, baby red potatoes, Nova's favorite, and broccoli. Soon after dinner is done, we settle in the living room, Nova sitting on the floor between my legs as I sit on the edge of the couch, parting her hair in two for her signature pigtails. Playing on the TV before us is Moana 2 at a comfortable volume, loud enough to grab Nova's attention in between her coloring a page in her Black Girl Superheroes coloring book.

I'd just recapped the bottle of hair butter when my phone buzzed against the glass, reminding me that I had left it there since Nova arrived home. I didn't rush to answer it, letting the light dim out while I emulsify the butter in my hands and spread it evenly over the two sections of Nova's hair. The two-minute chime reminds me of the missed notification, and I reach over Nova's head to grab the phone.

Tevin: Yo, why did Nina pack Denzel's dinner tonight… Buttered chicken, fried rice…and charred broccolini?!?! She won't leave the broccolini alone, huh? 😂

I giggle to myself, picturing the attempt my girl made to feed her man.

Me: Not too much on my girl! At least she's trying to keep her man fed. Not everyone can be a bomb cook like me.

Tevin: You're right. If you ever fall off, just feed me that juicy peach you're sitting on. I'll stay full for life! 😈

Me: Your ass so nasty. 😜

Tevin: 😈

"Oh, my God," I gawk aloud and then giggle. I put my phone to sleep and place it beside me on the couch, returning to Nova's hair.

"That's a different laugh," Nova observes, still coloring.

I squint my eyes, thrown off by her observation. Looping a band over one of her parts, I ask, "What are you talking about, boops?"

"Your laugh! It's different. Like…girly." I belt out a short laugh, still confused yet amused. Nova giggles quietly, still steadily coloring as she reads me. "See! That's your goofy laugh."

"Girl, that don't make any sense!" I exclaim, settling into a chuckle. "I don't have multiple laughs."

Nova scoots up so that she can turn to me and insists, "You do, Mommy. Your goofy laugh is like this…" Nova titters a laugh almost identical to mine and slaps her knee, and then abruptly falls into a neutral expression. She points at me, "That laugh you just did, it's girrrllyy." She elongates "girly" and then proceeds to mimic my laugh. It was high and chirpy like a hummingbird, and when she fluttered her eyes and twirled her fingers through the loose section of her hair, not in a band, I died laughing.

"You did!" Nova squeals, her laughter teetering through the air again. "You sound like you're laughing at a booooyyyy."

I gasp, stunned even further by how much she is picking up. I tap Nova's shoulder, a subtle signal for her to sit back, and she does. I continue with securing her second pigtail, thinking over my words before I speak them.

"Well…what if Mommy has a friend that makes her laugh…a boy?"

I feel my body tense slightly, waiting for her response. Nova has never seen or heard about any man in my life besides her father, and I had no idea what her response would be like. Would she be receptive to the idea of me being with someone who isn't her father? Would she feel like I'm putting her aside because I introduce someone into my life? Would she want to share me with someone else?

She shrugs nonchalantly. "I like it when you laugh, Mommy. You should let the boy keep making you laugh."

I huff a quiet laugh as I fluff out her pigtails, settled and satisfied by her simple approval. It was enough for me to feel like maybe it wouldn't be a bad idea to let her meet the one who makes me laugh and feel something I hadn't felt in a long time.

"Okay, group, we're on to the Space exhibit. Stay close!"

Even with my earphones on, I hear Miss Darby's voice. I hang back, letting the rest of the kids go before me so I can watch the colorful shadows dance against the wall, reflected by the mirror thing on an exhibit. But not too long—they are moving fast.

Today is my favorite day of summer camp. It's our last day, and we are on a field trip to Lovey's Bay Science Museum. I love the science museum. There are so many fun games and cool facts about animals, lights, and weather. I am excited to get to the weather room, but I'm trying to be patient. We've been doing everything except going there, but we are close. I can tell because as we walk, we pass by a picture of a tornado with the word

'WEATHER' written and an arrow pointing in the direction we were going. I almost ran into Paige because I'm so excited that we are close to the weather room.

EERRRHHH! EERRRHHH! EERRRHHH!

The screeching sound is so loud I freeze, whipping my head from side to side, trying to figure out what's happening. I pull my headphones from my ears, and the sound gets louder, making my insides shake.

"Fire alarm activated. Please find your way to the exit. Fire alarm activated. Please find your way to the exit."

"Okay, guys! Stay calm and follow the green arrows!"

I hear Miss Darby, but I can't make out where she is…or my classmates. Bright, white lights at the top of the ceiling are flashing on and off like a flashlight, and then, everyone around me is moving fast, zig-zagging. I pinch my eyes closed, feeling dizzy from everything. My heart is pounding so fast, and I try to take a deep breath to calm down, but when I open my eyes, I know that second to try to get myself together was a bad idea. I didn't see Miss Darby or anyone I recognized.

I dart my eyes to the floor to find the green arrows I heard Miss Darby mention. They're everywhere—pointing left, right, and straight. It doesn't help that people are stepping on them and following different green arrows. Which arrow am I supposed to follow? I look up, quickly looking for signs to show me where to go. Two red ones hang above…maybe they're a way out? They shouldn't be hard for me to figure out, but the letters swim together.

Exit? Exist?

"Oh, no…not now…" I whimper, but not loud enough for anyone to hear over the blaring alarm and people zipping past me. I fill my chest with air and try to choose a direction, but my feet won't let me. They stay planted as my body tries to jerk me in one way, then the other, until my legs finally release and carry me to the right…towards the Weather exhibit.

I feel different when I step into the Weather room. My eyes widen at all the sights. There are puffy white and gray clouds lining the ceiling, a big round light that looks like the sun, and then there's this empty open display in front of a wall painted with a swirling grey and black tornado. There's no one in the room, and inside, I know I probably shouldn't be here, especially with the alerts still going off, but I have to take a closer look at the tornado wall. This is what I wanted to see. I heard there's a live-action tornado display here, but from what I saw— a big empty square box with a fan in the middle —it didn't look like something a tornado would come from. I lean forward, looking down and observing the fan, trying to make sense.

Woosh!

"Ahh!"

I'm knocked back by a blast of cool air and then rapidly swirling smoke. When I stumble back, I collide with the sharp edge of something, trip over my feet, hit the ground, and then my glasses go flying off.

"Noooo…" I groan as I piano my hands across the floor like it's a keyboard, trying to locate my favorite glasses. All I feel is the cold floor, and when I look around, everything is blurry, including what I now know is the tornado display I was looking for. The display didn't matter anymore. My blurred vision is beginning to get murky as the tears well in my eyes, and my chest hurts from how hard I'm breathing. The emergency feels real now. I'm alone, and I don't know how I will find my way out.

"Okay, Kian, you gotta remember, your vision may be blurred in a real-life situation. Close your eyes. Now, how are you going to navigate through the hallway?"

The crew of five others encourages Kian as he hesitates for a beat and then begins to feel the plank in front of him before he starts moving with determination. I want to tell him to relax, but that hesitation looks like a habit, so I let him live. In a real-life situation, I want my crew to be able to handle any situation like pros. I make a mental note to pull him aside later and give him some constructive criticism.

"Aight, Maya, help your guy out," I instruct, nodding Maya to follow Kian through the desolate hall and call out warnings for any obstructions he comes across. For the rest of the drill, I stand back and observe what they've learned while low-key struggling to keep sleep in the background of my thoughts.

It's Friday, my official first day off from my shift with Company 143, but per usual, it's also training day with V-Squad. I don't know what it is, but something urged me to ask Denzel for permission to take the crew out to Smokestack, our training tower. We call it Smokestack because legend has it that the tower that still stands was the only portion of an old shipyard warehouse that remained standing after a massive fire. The story that's passed down is that when the fire crew finally got a hold of the blaze, the tower stood amongst the stack, solid and billowing thick black smoke. The city let the Fire Department take ownership of the tower, and as a result, it's been repurposed and reconstructed for our training purposes.

Denzel agreed with no pushback but was rather impressed with the suggestion.

"Yeah, that's a progressive idea," I remember Denzel complimenting, shaking his head enthusiastically. "Great way to prepare the crew for the potential for the real thing."

The real thing he spoke of is a real emergency, like an emergency that would call for them to assist one of the fire companies if more hands were needed. That's precisely why I suggested it. After a while, I stopped seeing the squad as degenerates and started calling them what they were: my team. Denzel doesn't step in with planning for them; he leaves it all up to me, and that had to be worth something. So, I started treating this like I was the Captain and began training them like they were professionally paid firefighters. Well, the few that treated the volunteer work like it was important to them. Maya, Kian, and Jace were always part of that number, unless they had personal obligations.

I take a long breath of the salt air floating through a light breeze, feeling accomplished while I watch the crew finish the drill. They've really caught on quickly and look like a team ready for anything. I'm ready to call drills early when alerts start ping-ponging between my phone and the crew's phones. I go to pull my phone when the dispatch radio gives off a two-tone, and then Denzel's voice comes through.

"What up, D," I answer, simultaneously pressing the side button to speak as I bring the radio to my mouth.

"Yeah, we need you and the squad at the science museum. Not quite sure what the emergency is, but we need hands to make sure everyone is evacuated. You think your crew can handle it?"

I shake my head as if he can see me. "Fasho. Rolling out now."

"Copy that."

The radio chirps again, this time alerting that Denzel is no longer on the other side. Attaching the radio back to my hip, I make long strides towards the crew who stood there waiting for my confirmation. Clapping my hands together, I bark enthusiastically, "Playtime's over, V-Squad! It's showtime! Let's go!"

The scene isn't exactly the showtime I expect. When the V-Squad and I walk into Lovey's Bay Science Museum, it looks like the ending of a show with people straggling out from different directions toward the exit. There's no smoke, not even a faint smell of it in the air, only blaring alarms echoing through the museum. When my disappointed glare meets Denzel's eyes, he puts his hands up.

"We're still trying to figure out what happened here," he explains. "The call came in because the fire alarm went off, but no one could identify why. We haven't yet either, but there are some reports that some have seen smoke or smelled it…" Denzel shrugs. "Nothing's clear yet. The only thing clear is that we have guests still roaming the museum, and we need to get them out while our guys check for any dangers."

I'm slightly disappointed in the lack of action, but I only let it show through a sigh before I say, "Okay. We're on it then."

Denzel nods, releasing a sigh of his own, his filled

with relief. "Great. One more thing. We have a missing kid—a little girl. There are a ton of summer camps here today, and they lost the girl when the alarms went off. She's about seven or eight and was last seen on the second floor in the Reflection exhibit. While you guys point people to the exit, keep an eye out for the girl."

"Got it," I say, dapping Denzel before he trots away. I turn to my crew, whose eyes meet me, eager for orders. I repeat the information given to me by Denzel and then split my crew up into pairs to take on the large museum. Before dismissing them, I give them a pep talk. "I know this isn't an emergency like what we trained for today, but it's still important. We have an unknown emergency at hand, and it's our duty to make sure the people are safe. They count on us, and I'm counting on you, V-Squad. Don't forget to use your radios if you need anything."

We split up, with Kian and Maya heading straight ahead, two of my other volunteers going to the hall to the left, and Jace and me heading to the right towards the stairs. I take the steps two at a time with Jace's boots clunking not too far behind me against the marble flooring.

"Why are there still so many people just wandering around like there aren't alarms going off?" Jace's question comes after we reach the second floor and are met by a group of guests still wandering like it's a normal day at the museum. Politely, we ask them to leave before I shrug, answering his rhetorical question.

"Hell if I know. People don't believe in an emergency unless they see smoke or blood."

Jace walks beside me through the reflection room and snorts, "Shit, that's all truths right there. I guess that's how the little girl was forgotten."

"No, that's just irresponsible," I grumble, scanning my eyes over the corners, remembering we had a missing child to look for.

"Watch we find her in the gift shop or something," Jace jokes.

My eyes go to a sign reading "Weather" and curiously I head that way, mumbling, "That would be ideal."

But it isn't where we find the little girl. As I enter the room full of different weather scenarios, a small frame is in front of us on the ground. I recognize the sandy brown pig tails and pink headphones hanging from her neck as she swipes her hand across the floor like she's reading braille. I'm confused as I watch and notice she's murmuring with a slight whimper. I scan the grounds for what she might be looking for, my irises landing on pink glasses. That's when it dawns on me.

"Nova?"

At the sound of her name, she stops moving and sits up on her shins. She squints and looks around. Her face constricts, and I can see the streaks on her cheek glistening, evidence of her crying. I take quick steps towards her, grabbing her glasses as I close in on her.

"Supernova," I say, this time my tone calm and more familiar. I can see her gasp and then exhale as if she recognizes my voice, but her face still shows her fear. I kneel in front of her and unfold her glasses. "Here, let me help you see."

Gently, I slide her glasses onto her face, tucking each leg of the glasses behind her ear and out of the way of her hair. Nova blinks rapidly and then looks up at me with those big doe eyes just like her mom's. Her face softens as she recognizes me. I marvel over her features, forgetting for a moment where I am. It's like I'm seeing her for the first time, although it isn't the first time. This time, however, I have the opportunity to really look at her. She looks so much like Joni. The features I love the most about Joni are making up Nova's features. The only feature I never want to see on hers or Joni's face again is the despair that still settles within her glossy eyes.

"Mr. Tevin," she squeaks, finally fully realizing who I am, the firefighter from school. And as Joni's face shines through hers, it hits me harder that it's Nova, the side of Joni I've been waiting to really get to know. She sucks in short, stammering breaths as she explains, "I-I got confused by the signs…and…and then the tornado went off and I fell..and..and…"

I place a soothing hand on her shoulder, prompting

her words to fail as she looks up at me. I smile and assure her, "Hey. It's all good, Supernova. What matters is I found you." The corner of her mouth tics into a half smile as she exhales and calms. "Are you okay? Did you hurt yourself when you fell?"

"No," she whines. She touches her side and winces a little. "I just hit my side on something sharp."

I look past her, identifying what she possibly collided with: a square edge of another display. It wasn't super sharp, but I could see how it may have caused the pain in her side.

"Hey, what do you say I carry you out? You know, Superman helping a Superstar out?"

She snuffles as she nods her permission and then reaches her hands for me. I scoop her up, comfortably placing her on my side as she wraps her arm around my neck.

We emerge from the museum into the sun-beating outdoors, greeted with applause from the Fire Crew. Fire trucks line the circular drop-off with people scattered in clumps throughout the parking lot. Denzel walks up and stands on the opposite side of me, looking between me and Nova.

"Hey, Nova," Denzel greets warmly and in an octave

three times higher than his usual baritone. He tugs at a pigtail, making her giggle.

"Mr. Denzel. It's you!" she greets back, taking me aback at how well they know each other.

"Yeah, baby girl. I wish I had known you were missing. You okay?"

"Yes, I'm fine. Mr. Tevin found me. I got confused with the signs…" Her words trail off again, and I can tell she's really bent out of shape about the signs, but I don't quite understand.

"It's okay, baby girl," Denzel expresses. "Signs can be tricky, especially in an emergency. Great thing is you're okay, right?" She nods, and then Denzel moves his eyes to me, speaking lower. "You know…?"

"Not really," I answer, cutting him off. I know what he's asking without having to say. After I put things on ice with Joni and me, I've griped to him and Deacon about not knowing the side of Joni that included Nova. What I didn't tell him is that I met her during the volunteer day at the elementary school. Deacon squints his eyes in puzzle and I shake my head. "Long story."

Denzel slowly nods his understanding. "Well, her mother is eager to see her."

He bows his head as his eyes look past me. I can hear Joni before I turn to see her.

"How the hell do you lose a child?!"

The wrath coming from Joni is one I didn't ever want to be on the other end of. I felt bad for the lady, but not completely, because Joni is right: How do you lose a kid? I start walking in her direction with Nova still in my arms, hoping to save the woman, but my steps falter slightly as I see a man step up beside Joni and place a comforting hand on her shoulder. Joni violently shrugs him off her shoulder, and I snickered only for it to be stifled by Nova's screech.

"Mommy! Daddy!"

Hearing Nova's voice, Joni's head spins, and then she takes off towards us. The guy lags a step behind Joni.

"Nova, baby!" Joni reaches up as Nova leans into her and pulls her close into an embrace.

For a moment, it's only her and Nova as she peppers kisses all over her giggling face. It was almost like a That's so Raven moment when it hits Joni that they aren't alone, and then she looks up at me. Her pupils grow big, soften, and then swell with something else before she pops onto the balls of her heels and pulls my face into her hands to kiss me.

It doesn't matter to me that I'm on the clock or that there are people around watching the scene, including the man I found out is Nova's dad. I pull my lady into me and tongue her down while Nova squirms, giggles, and ewws.

"Eww, Mommy!"

Joni pecks my lips before pulling away and touching

her own, her eyes moving from one side to the other, observing those looking before she looks to Nova and giggles quietly.

Nova cackles, almost identical to Joni's goofy laugh. "See, Mommy! I told you that laugh is because of a boyyyy!"

JONI

"Okay, no one loses or gains any weight over the next two months," Nina warns. She ambles in front of Fallon, me, and the three other women who are her bridesmaids, pointing her finger at each one of us like a drill sergeant.

"That goes for you, too. No weight and no babies!" Nina turns to me and I fold my lips into each other, stifling my laugh after my remark, but Fallon blows through her puffed cheeks and the rest of the ladies fall in line. I break character.

Nina folds her arms across her chest, trying to hold back her laugh. "Just so you know, I have lost five pounds, and Denzel and I have gone celibate until the wedding."

"What?"

"Celibate?"

"Girl….ain't no kind of way…!" I blurt out, throwing my hands up and shaking my head.

"Tuh, tell me about it," Fallon adds, slapping one of my raised hands. "Deacon and I smashed before the wedding."

I catch her hand before she pulls away, closing in the five. "You horny toads. You ain't even supposed to see him before the wedding!"

"I'm not supposed to see him in my wedding dress. I wasn't in my dress."

Fallon and I burst into laughter, loud and messy, like Regina King and Jackee Harry's drunken time on *Watch What Happens Live*. Everyone around us cackles like they are our audience as we disperse to our dressing rooms, removing the various styles of champagne gold gowns.

I managed to persuade Vashti to extend the store hours at Love x Lace just for Nina's bridesmaid fitting tonight. It wasn't a hard ask, considering Nina's bridal party consists of six bridesmaids who were all purchasing gowns and accessories from the boutique, enough to cover two overtime hours of pay for Whitney and Jemma, one of our sales associates. Besides, I'm present, which means she didn't have to come in to close the boutique afterwards. I assured her that I would stay and make sure everything is done right. But, until closing time, Whitney and Jemma make sure I don't lift a finger, besides my pinky finger to signal I want more champagne. At first, I found it hard to let go of control, but after a glass, and then a second, of champagne, I can say I'm gone with the wind fabulous. At this point, at the tail end of the fitting, we were all very much woozy from the bubbly libation and having probably way too much fun trying on our dresses.

"It's really not that hard," Nina reiterates after a few more jokes and gawks went around about her celibacy. "Besides, we wanted it to feel like the first time again on our wedding night."

"How sway?!" I call out, coercing more giggles from the party. We are now lounging in the display room, taking up the tufted benches and chairs scattered around. "He's been all up and through you, and you've had a whole child."

"Wait," Fallon slurs, putting up a wobbly finger. "The real question is, how long has it been since you two started the celibacy?"

Nina crosses her legs as she lounges back in her chair, her chin lifted as she confidently replies, "We're up two weeks now."

Fallon downs the last of the golden liquid in her champagne chute before she tilts her head to Nina and purses her lips, giving her a short, unagreeable, "Mm."

"Whatever, Fallon. Unlike you, I can control the patter of my pussy."

"Oop!" I hiccup, bugging my eyes at Nina's unusually uncouth response. I move my eyes to Fallon, who's now lying on her back on the lounge chair she occupies. She kicks up her leg, causing the skirt of the dress to bunch around her upper thigh, and wiggles her toes.

"No, I don't control it. Deacon does…and he keeps it pat-pat-pat—"

Fallon is now gyrating her hips to the rhythm of her words, and the room comes alive again. Nina gets up and playfully swats at Fallon's exposed thigh. "Oh, my Gosh, Fallon! Will you cool it already?! You talking about sex is not helping this mission!"

The two playfully swat at each other before falling into a clumsy hug, Nina nearly taking both of them off the lounge chair.

"Okaayy. On that note, last call for alcohol!" Whitney announces, strolling into the room with the last of the two bottles of champagne in her hands. She has them raised above her head like a true bottle girl. She tops off everyone with what looks like a splash each as the room settles again.

"All jokes aside, I'm so happy for you, Nina," Fallon says, pulling herself upright. She raises her glass to Nina. "I was a little nervous you were going to scare that man away, catching everything in sight on fire."

We cackle at Nina's expense, and I even heard a few "Mmhmm" from the bridal party. Nina bunches her lips and narrows her eyes at Fallon before sticking her tongue out at her.

I jump in. "But our girl got her man, even after I had to tell her ass to stop playing double dutch with Denzel's feelings."

Nina puts her hand up and shifts to look at me. "Nuh-uh. Stop it. I did not play with Denzel's feelings. I just had some things to let go of." I dip my head towards her, piercing her with disbelief. Nina scoffs. "I did, and I let them go, hence why I have my man now. The real question is, when are you and Tevin going to stop playing hide and go freak and just be together? We all know y'all have a thing!"

My jaw drops. "First is 'pattering pussy', now 'hide and go freak?' You've had enough for the night."

Playfully, I go to take the champagne flute from Nina's hand. She snatches her arm from my grasp, spilling some of the sip she has left, and nearly loses her balance on the edge of the lounge chair. Fallon grabs her arm, steadying her before giggling at the scene.

"To be fair, I think Joni locked down her man the other day," Fallon exposes. She wiggles her eyebrows at me. "That kiss said, 'Don't nobody talk about my mama or my mannnn!"

Fallon transforms her voice to mimic the reality

goddess, Nene Leakes, in her comical rendition of Kandi's remark in a classic Real Housewives of Atlanta episode. The impression didn't fly over anyone's head, and the room broke out in laughter again. As for me, my chuckle comes out choppy through my tight bashful smile.

Nina turns to me, her eyes round and curious. "What kiss and why does Fallon know before me?"

I open my mouth to correct…explain…shit, I didn't know what to say about my spontaneous display of affection the day Nova got lost in the museum. Fallon assisted, but in a way that had the ladies cooing.

"I only know because I was on duty…and so was he. We had a call come in from the science museum on Saturday. Some kid pulled the fire alarm as a prank, but no one knew at the time. We also had a missing child. Nova. Guess who found her? *Lover boy Tevin.* Guess who slobbered him? *Juicy lips Joni!*"

As everyone carried on like an audience watching a romantic scene live, I threw back the last of my champagne. I'm not sure if the flush of heat through my body is from the champagne or the thought of the kiss.

I didn't "slobber" Tevin down, but I didn't stop our kiss from intensifying. I had only pecked him, being immersed in all the feelings that swarmed me. There was elation that my baby girl was found, and when I realized it was Tevin whom she clung to, the feeling submerged with everything that felt right.

The kiss felt right in the moment, and so did him slipping his tongue into my mouth in front of everybody. His crew. Nova and the gawking children. Malik.

"That's a whole week, and I'm just finding out all this juicy info!" Nina counts on her fingers and then pins me with squinted eyes.

"This is the first time I'm hearing about it, too," Whitney chimes in. She stands leaning against the door-less hinge between the display and the front room. "No wonder the flowers from Avery have slowed down."

"Okay, so can everyone stop spilling *my business*?!" I protest, waving my hands and giggling. "Nina, I didn't say anything because I didn't think it was that big of a deal. Like you said, everybody knows Tevin and I have a…thing."

A thing. It's the only way I can explain what Tevin and I have because we've never classified what we do as anything, even though the night we shared after Nova's rescue felt like we had something more than just "a thing." It felt like something along the lines of a real connection. Like it wasn't just sex we indulged in after Nova was sound asleep in her room. It felt like our hearts were involved. The way he kissed my most sensitive points and depths. The way I clung to his back as he plummeted my sopping walls. The way our mouths locked as we came undone together….it felt like so much more than a thing.

Fallon snorts and inserts her two cents again. "You can lie to yourself if you want, but I'm going to tell you the truth. That kiss didn't look like you two have just a thing."

"It never looks like you two are just 'a thing," Nina concurs. "You two aren't fooling anybody—maybe yourselves, but even I don't buy that. Just be together already so we can prepare for another wedding!"

The crew sends a muttered agreement to Nina's remark, including the bridesmaids who were only privy to the little information Nina and Fallon spilled about my business, before everyone begins moving around to prepare to end the fitting session. Nina and Fallon's words echo in my mind as I start to jump into my managerial duties. Perhaps we were the only ones muddled behind the smoke of our unspoken words, while the whole time we were mirroring something even our friends could see.

TEVIN

"This might be the second year in a row where it's been quiet for the 4th."

I lean back in the recliner, thinking about Deacon's statement, then straighten up, looking across the folding table decorated with playing cards to him. We are sitting in the station's lounge and have just finished a game of spades on a hella chill Saturday just before the 4th of July holiday. The area is roughly the size of our living room, furnished with a big screen TV, a couple of sofas, and the recliner I'm sitting in. Since it's a quiet night, we decide to pull out the folding chair and set up for a game or two. We just finished game two, with Deacon and Denzel winning the second game. Joss and I won the first, with Jace and Maya hanging out for the night, watching.

"You know, you might be right about that. The last

time we had a catastrophic night was when you and Denzel were on duty and the freak accident happened at Nina's." I look to Denzel with mischief written all over my face. "Maybe having Nina under your supervision is the key to our easy holiday."

The table of six roars in laughter. Deacon tries not to give in to a full laugh for the sake of his homie, but Joss, Maya, and Jace crack up, having heard about Denzel's accident-prone fiancée.

"Aight, now. Leave the Misses alone," Denzel grumbles yet chuckles, being a good sport about it. "It's about time she gets off your list of jokes."

I bug my eyes at him. "Shiiiit! We just had to save her from scorching herself and her dress!"

"Oh, shit, he's right," Joss says, sitting back in her folding chair. She clasps her hand over her mouth, trying to stifle her laugh. The rest of the crew at the table wasn't so respectful. "Man, my bad. I know that's your lady, but damn, Chief. Is she that bad at home?"

I open my mouth to answer, but Denzel cuts his eye at me as he responds, "No. She's…better now."

"Now?" Maya asks, her eyes showering her bewilderment. The table cracks again, mouthing a silent "I'm sorry" to Denzel while falling into Joss's shoulder, laughing.

Denzel continues shaking his head while gathering the cards. "Look, can we stop deflecting from this game

Deacon and I are whoopin' y'all asses in?" He slides the messy stack to me. "It's your turn to shuffle. And don't cheat."

"Man, when have I ever cheated?" I ask, twisting my mouth at him as I gather the cards into a neat stack.

"Mm, I can think of one time," Deacon murmurs, his smirk hanging devilishly to the right side.

I suck my teeth. "When? I ain't never had to cheat to win a spades game. I stay dustin' y'all old asses."

"Lie," Deacon rebuts. He leans his elbow onto the table, deadpanning at me. "You don't remember that time you went on a date with another woman. Like, two weeks ago?"

I'm mid-response when I pause. "Funny, but I'd never cheat on my 'Big Booty Judy, ' but Joni and I aren't together, so that was nothing."

I hear Jace make a noise of uncertainty, and I turn to my left, seeing him scratching his head. "I haven't been around that long, but I can't tell she's not your girl."

"Wait. Are y'all talking about the chick Tevin tackled at the beach?" Maya asks, moreso directing his question to Jace.

Joss bumps her shoulder against Maya, grabbing her attention. "She's the mom of the little girl he found at the museum. You know, the one he was playing tonsil hockey with."

There's a moment between Maya and Joss, I peep

where Joss wets her bottom lip while bouncing her eyes from Maya's lips to her eyes. It's gone just as quickly as it came when Maya breaks the moment by shifting her wide eyes to me. "Oooh, I know! Yeah, that's the chick from the beach. I don't know, Cappi, you either lying or about to catch a case, because the way you had her hemmed up at the museum…"

Their agreement and laughter blend with the slap of the cards as I cut and shuffle them. "I'm not lying, and I'm not catching a case. What's understood between me and Joni is just that."

It's just that I don't know what's understood between us now. We are back in the swing of our old thing again, but it feels different. I've met Nova, but not exactly how I thought I would, but I did, and Joni didn't clam up about it. Shit, it was her that initiated the kiss in front of Nova and then, in so many words that a kid could understand, told her I was her "friend." I'll take that, because that's what I am, but I want more. I think she wants more, too, just based on how things unfolded after the museum incident.

I stopped by hours after the scene was cleared at the museum. I could've called, but Nova's frightened face kept flashing in my head, and my chest was still tingling from the surprise kiss from Joni. I didn't expect to stay. I was fully prepared to stand outside of her apartment and inquire if Nova had settled in for the night well and make sure Joni was good, too, but she invited me in.

Questions of well-being turned into me checking her body for tension, and like a good lover, easing it out. Except that the sex wasn't just sex like in the past. It felt more intimate. It felt like we were both in this deeper than we are letting on to each other.

The third game kicks off, and as I expect, Joss retakes the lead by a book. Ready to collect our next book, Deacon and Denzel slow down the collection with a long pause, obviously trying to talk through their ogling eyes.

"Aight, if y'all gotta take this long, you ain't got it," I tease. It doesn't make the two move any faster, so I pull out my phone.

Me: Y'all still prancing around in dresses?

Joni: Nope. I'm home now…sulking in my loneliness. 😭

I note the time, and it's almost ten at night.

Me: No after drinks?

Joni: Nope. I think we had enough at the boutique. They had to call rideshares for Nina and Fallon. Don't tell the guys. 😂

Me: Pause. How the hell you get home?

I snicker as I look up at Deac and Denzel. Deacon finally places his card down, making it clear they had nothing for that hand. Slamming my hand on the table, I boast, "Got 'em! Now give us our damn books!"

"Yeah, yeah. It's just one book. Let me go get something to drink real quick," Deacon grumbles as Joss grabs the books.

As Deacon pushes away from the table, the chair legs screeching against the concrete floor, I add salt to the insult. "Yeah, get something to quench that thirst for a win you got."

Deacon calls over his shoulder, "You talkin' a lot of shit for a youngin' that just started winnin', Tevin No-Cambell."

I laugh off his sour joke and return to my phone.

Joni: I didn't drive. Whitney brought me home. I could've drove, though. My buzz wore off by the time I finished helping them close.

Me: That's what they all say. Glad Whit brought you home. I wish I could keep you company.

Joni: Yeah, me too, but I'll be okay. I just miss Nova. A lot. I'm like this every summer she goes away with her dad. Hopefully I won't be in my feelings for half the time she's gone…lol.

I sit with her words, my brain already coming up with a way to pull Joni out of her feelings. For as long as I've known Joni, I could tell Nova was her whole world, and I can see how her being gone more than three days could make her feel more lonely than usual. I just didn't know last year she had been in her feelings for half the time she was gone.

Me: You still off until Tuesday?

Joni: Yeah. Why?

Me: Pack a small suitcase. Swimsuit. Something chill. Something nice. Be ready for me to scoop you at 9 am.

I watch the dots dance on the screen, and I know Joni is over there trying to come up with some excuse.

Joni: Tevin, you get off at 8 am. Where do you think you're taking me with no sleep?

I snicker, knowing I was right with my assumption.

Me: Don't worry about all that. We aren't going too far. Just be ready. Okay?

This time, there's no dancing dots on the screen. Just me waiting for Joni's confirmation.

.   .   .

"You done boo-lovin' yet so we can get back to this game?" I look up at Joss, who smirks and nods her head to the table where Deacon is back and ready to play. My phone pings, and I look down.

Joni: Okay then.

Content, I place my phone on the table, pick up my cards, and smirk, "I am now."

22

JONI

Just like he said, Tevin is at my door at nine sharp. And like he asked, I am ready. When I open the door, he stands there with no signs that he'd just worked a 24-hour shift: no bloodshot eyes or sleep-deprived bags. The only giveaway is the blue sweats stamped with the fire company logo at the hip. He pairs them with a white undershirt, white classic Jordans, and a black durag stylishly tied. When he pulls me in for a hug before taking my bag, I can smell the fresh, spicy custom-blended scent of his body wash, cologne, and deodorant. He smells irresistible. Without warning, I feel the seat of my panties moistening. I shift in my hips, internally embarrassed at how quickly and easily he turns me on.

What am I doing? Where are we going?

The questions bounce through my mind the whole drive from my apartment and down the coastal highway, lining Lovey's Bay Beach. Tevin doesn't volunteer a concise answer either when I decide to vocalize my questions.

"Just sit back and ride," he answers, giving me a cursory glance and a wink before returning his eyes to the road. "We're not going far."

That's the only clue he gives me for the entire twenty minutes of our drive. When I realize that our destination is only twenty minutes away, I almost feel bamboozled. I stayed up past midnight last night rummaging through my closet to find a swimsuit or two, something nice, and something chill. For a woman, 'something nice' and 'something chill' could mean anything from sundresses to date-night outfits. I packed four of each and two swimsuits. But when we passed the weathered wooden sign reading, The Coves, my breath got caught in my chest, and my feelings changed. I've never been to this side of Lovey's Bay, and I drink in every sight we pass— the gated entrances to several neighborhoods, the hyper-pigmented green landscaping and sky-high palm trees, the glimpses of the calm waves of the private beach area of Lovey's Bay that peak through the multi-million dollar properties.

We eventually veer off the coastal highway-turned-two-lane street onto a road on the right. It leads us into a quaint neighborhood of beach house cottages, their minimal landscaping marked by long, pointy grass. Many of them were one-story homes, yet screamed money simply because of their location.

Our destination is a cottage-style beach house with a weathered, pale wooden walkway. The morning sun beams onto the house, making the blue paneling and white trim even brighter. There's a soft wind blowing, swaying the pointy grass lightly.

"Welcome to your staycation," Tevin announces once he shuts off the engine. I twist my head to him as my smile crests over my lips. Almost seeming to be reactive to mine, Tevin's gorgeous smile quirks to the side, revealing a glimpse of his pearly whites. "I thought you could use a little pick-me-up getaway."

"Tevin, are you serious?" I breathe, my words floating between disbelief and swooning as I look past him to the cottage.

"We're here, aren't we? How serious can that be?" Tevin's questions are playful and don't actually warrant a response. Besides, the only thing I can muster is a giggle and a "Thank you" before I reach over the console and pull him by his ears to me to kiss him. There's a spark that sets off at the touch of our lips, ushering away the somberness that once settled in my chest because of Nova's absence. What replaces it is a subtle reminder by way of a classic line from the movie Baby Boy, coming from Jody's mom, Juanita: "Mama's gotta have a life too."

A satisfied moan rumbles in his throat before he pecks my lips and pulls back with desiring eyes. "Anything for you, babe."

It took no more than thirty minutes after getting settled inside the cottage for Tevin to conk out. One minute, he was talking to me while I explored the en suite bathroom, taking in the sunken jacuzzi-style tub and separate rainfall shower. Next, I walked back into the bedroom and found him stretched out on his stomach, quietly snoring. I knew he had to be tired, so I didn't bother him, besides carefully sliding his sneakers off his feet. The distant squawk of seagulls pulls my attention to the glass and wood-framed double doors to my right. The doors open up to a deck, and curiously, I tiptoe over to check out the view.

Immediately upon pushing the doors open, the salty and humid air accosts me, and then the smooth breeze, balancing it all out. The deck stretches the length of the house. To the east side, there's a grill set up with a prep shelf beside it and an L-shape wicker sectional topped with white cushions. A table sits in front of the couch, and near the end of the deck, a dining set with a few chairs faces the ocean. Tucked in the corner is a sunken jacuzzi. I snicker to myself—it's clear the owners have a thing for Jacuzzis. I make a mental note to test it out later.

What really set off the deck vibes is that it faces Lovey's Bay Beach. I step further onto the deck and stop in front of the railing enclosing the deck, looking over the view. Lovey's Bay is beautiful, but this side feels like a different coast. The water is a bright turquoise and nearly clear, in contrast to the dark, blue-green water I'm used to in the area nearest my apartment. And on the sandy beach, there are fresh tracks, evidence of the sand being leveled and manicured this morning. I guess that's the difference between areas with more affluence than others: they had more money to spend on making the beach feel aesthetically pleasing, like you're somewhere besides Greenbrook.

I look over my shoulder back into the dim room to a still slumbering Tevin. He's moved onto his side with his back facing me. He looks like he'll be out for a while. Meanwhile, my mind is counting down the hours I have left before I have to return to my reality. Without a second thought, I kick off my slip-on sandals and skip down the wooden pathway towards the beach. I'm not necessarily dressed for a frolic on the beach, wearing denim jean shorts and a white cropped tank top, but I didn't care. I jog through the cool, grainy sand and then over the moist sand until I'm immersed in the cool water to my waist. An incoming wave causes the water to rise above my chest and splash my face. The shock of the water's crispness and the thrill of being fully clothed in it elicit a yelp and giggle. I let go of any lingering tension as I relax and float along with the waves, tilting my head up to let the sun bathe my face. Tevin's face fades in from the back of my eyelids, and I don't know if the warmth that spreads through my body is from the sun or from the feeling of being seen by Tevin.

I didn't really say much, but he was able to pick up what I needed: a vacation away and a reprieve to take off my mommy vest. Not only did he realize it, but he also took action. I've never had anyone take action for the sake of my sanity and peace, but then again, I'd never let anyone as close to me as I have let Tevin since Malik and I broke up. This type of support feels good, and I wonder why it has taken me so long to realize this is what I've been missing.

"You deserve…" I whisper into the air as I pull in a breath, my eyes still closed to the sun. I let go even further, eventually floating on my back in the water. "I deserve it all."

. . .

As if the day couldn't get any more perfect, lounging in the jacuzzi watching the sunset is like the extra sweet layer of icing to my cake. As the sun creeps behind the horizon, the sky transforms to an amber-gold hue with a deep blue chasing close behind it. The beach is peaceful with only the sounds of the gentle waves crashing and seagull calls all day. I saw a few people on the beach during my visit earlier, but only a handful. Tonight, it sounds as if there is no one around at all, a sensory peace I can get used to.

I sink a little further into the bubbling, steamy water, resting my head against the brick base of the jacuzzi. Before closing my eyes, I stretch my right arm until my fingertips graze and wrap around the stem of my wine glass. The contrast of the chilled bubbly against my lips and the heated bubbles rolling over my body is a sensational combination that forces a soft moan from my lips. I hear Tevin's snicker from behind.

"You sound like you're having a whole lot of fun over there without me."

I sink my teeth into my bottom lip, stifling a slightly embarrassed blush back, but then shrug it off. "Maybe, maybe not."

"Damn," Tevin chuckles, persuading a giggle out of me. I flip over so that I'm facing him and prop my head on my hands, the wine glass still settled in my right.

Tevin carries a different allure about him as I watch

him at the grill. His back is away from me, giving me a view of the dip and curve of his back muscles with each subtle movement. My eyes roam down his back and to the swim trunks he wears. They hang enticingly low but cover his tight, muscular ass. Over the last year, Tevin's been putting in the gym, and it shows. I've never had a problem with his physique, but now, it makes my saliva as thick with desire.

Maybe it's the second glass of wine.

Maybe not.

The soft sizzle from the grill pulls me from my lustful thoughts. "What's for dinner?"

"Mm," he hums as he closes the lid to the grill. He turns to me. "Something light. Oysters, lobster, and summer squash and zucchini."

I lift an impressed eyebrow. "Fancy. I'm learning a lot about you today."

He snorts. "Like what?"

"Like you eat more than oodles and noodles, and you know about destinations like this."

I look over the deck for emphasis and then back at him. He snuffles and shakes his head. "You know damn well I don't eat that salty ass oodles and noodles."

Snickering, I admit, "That's true. But this...how'd you find out about this place? And don't say TikTok."

My remark brings a laugh straight from Tevin's belly. "I'm young, but I do not rely on TikTok for everything, damn. I'm a little cultured. I know how to find nice places like this when I need to."

"You must've brought one of your little girlfriends here before."

I sip from my glass again and cut my eye to him, waiting for his response. He tilts his head and twists his mouth at me before he ambles toward me. He kneels before me, bringing his face to mine. "No, I've never brought anyone here before. Just you. Trips like this are for the one and only special person in my life."

Tevin scans my eyes for understanding. The subtle confirmation of his feelings for me makes my stomach flutter and my lips part slightly. He holds me in his trance for a wave longer before pecking my lips and promptly standing up again, returning to the grill. His retreat is the ribbon unraveling my inner composure. I hope that it's a sign of me being completely undone by the night's end.

It's only about ten minutes before Tevin joins me in the jacuzzi with the accompaniment of a plate for us to share. The aroma of garlic and butter hits my nose before I see the plate between us, as he's floating in front of me. I eye the oyster suspiciously.

"I don't know about the oysters," I say, half admitting I've never had them before.

He gawks. "Don't tell me, seasoned Joni's never had oysters."

"Not too much on the seasoned, youngin'," I tease, narrowing my eyes at him. I continue to eye the oyster shell he picks up, focusing more on the gooey counterpart topped with liquid I assume is the butter and little specs of garlic.

"Well, let this youngin' expose you to something new." He places the plate on the edge of the jacuzzi, still holding the oyster in his right hand. Leveling it to my mouth, he closes in and pierces me with those persuading eyes again. "Do you trust me?"

My eyes turn into slits as I playfully ponder the question. Behind my playfulness, the truth that I trusted Tevin with my life lingers. "Yes. I trust you."

A smile ghosts his lips as he wets them. "Good. So, this is what I want you to do. Tilt back." I eye him, dubiously yet intrigued, and tilt my head back. He places the lukewarm shell to my lips. "Now, just swallow."

I know his direction isn't meant to be erotic, but that's where my mind went, especially when the thick and slimy contents slip down my throat. Just as quickly as it slides down, my nipples peak, and my center vibrates. When I bring my head back to level, Tevin is burning lust-filled holes in me, surely with the same thoughts that swam in my mind.

"Whatchu think?" he asks in a low, raspy voice.

I rub my lips together, feeling them moist from the butter and giving myself a moment to compose myself.

The energy between us had me ready to pounce on him and forget dinner.

"Mm," I hum with a slight rise in octave. "Reminds me of something I've done before."

Tevin throws his head back, sending his howling laughter through the air, before he meets my eyes again. I'm snickering now, pleased to have cut the tension...slightly. My walls were still pulsing with the want to feel him between them. It was enough to cool the heat between us for us to share the delicious meal he prepared for a short while.

All it takes is a flirty eye while I seductively place a buttered lobster meat into my mouth, letting my fingers slowly glide from my mouth. I watch Tevin watch each movement, from the disappearance and reappearance of my fingers to the running of my tongue across my lips. That's when he closes the space between us, placing a hand on either side of the jacuzzi edge. He licks at my bottom lip, now hanging from the shuddering breath that leaves me as the heat of his body engulfs me.

"You wasted a little something...right there," he whispers onto my lips before he pecks and licks at them again.

My hands wrap around his neck as I play along. "Did I?"

"Mmhmm," he hums before sliding his hands down my slick side.

He pecks again as he wraps his hands around my ass and squeezes a handful. A soft moan finds its way through my parted lips, allowing him to slip his tongue into my mouth. The kiss turns up a passionate notch almost immediately, making it evident that we both had been holding back our yearning for this moment. Our tongues thrash hungrily while our bodies dance against each other as if we could be any closer than we already were. The water slaps around us as soft moans fall between our kisses, and then I hiss as Tevin sucks on my bottom lip before wrapping his own around my neck. He flicks his tongue and kisses on the spot he knows pulls on the strings connected to my center. How does he find every button on my body? I don't know, but it is the most gratifying. He never misses and never forgets.

Tevin has a way with his tongue that he can use it on any part of my body and I could climax. I can feel the blood rushing through my body to its pending doom, but then gravity leaves me, and the cool contrast of the air against my wet body. I can't be happier for the shift. I needed an orgasm, but my body's begging for more.

"Fuck dinner. I got pussy to eat," Tevin groans as he sits me atop the jacuzzi edge.

"What?" I ask, while my legs part voluntarily. It's the only word my mind can formulate, still hazy from the shift and his quick pop of the strings of my swimsuit. I didn't need an answer. All I need is the impending feasting of my pussy that I am on the brink of.

"Lean back on your arms…I've been waiting on this all day…" I oblige as I feel the material of my bottoms slip from underneath me, and my shaky legs find rest on Tevin's shoulders. Then, my breath catches as he grazes my sensitive bulb between his teeth and then suction. A guttural moan leaves my body as he sucks and then rapidly flicks his tongue against my knob. He alternates between this and stroking my walls with his tongue, flattening and dragging between my folds, and doing a sucking kiss to my pearl. My body is in sensory overload. My right nipple is aching from the pluck and twist he does to it with his left hand. My legs convulse under the hold he has on the left with his right hand. My fingers on my right hand dig into the brick beneath me as I hold the back of Tevin's rotating head into my sopping pussy with my left. The water ripples softly as Tevin shifts. The salacious slurping of my juices pushes me closer to the edge. My whimpers are sirenic calls of pleasure when I come undone, bucking feverishly against his face, my nerve endings fire off in a tsunami of waves from my head to the tip of my curled toes.

I feel like I am spineless by the time I come down from my orgasm. Tevin has to support me with his arm hooked around my waist as he comes up to meet me face to face. When I flutter my eyes to him, sweat clings to his forehead while my juices smear his lips and chin. He leans in and I kiss him, letting his tongue transfer my taste to my mouth.

In between languid kisses, Tevin pauses, staring at me with dreamy eyes. In a raspy whisper, he reveals, "Now that tops my list of the best meal I've ever had."

23

TEVIN

"**S**o how did you meet Nova exactly?"

I peel my eyes open at the sound of Joni's question. She's lying on my chest, her naked body tangled in mine. We share the mangled king-sized sheet, crumpled like a tissue, and mostly covering Joni. It's bunched and covering her breast down to the cups of her ass, while as for me, a small portion of the sheet covers my manhood. The sun hasn't quite risen yet, and I am on my way back to sleep after nudging Joni away for a morning session when she asks the random question.

I shift so that I am angled to look down at her comfortably. "Uhh, the V-Squad had a volunteer event at the school before summer break. It just so happened that we were volunteering with Nova's class that day."

Joni remains silent, and I assume she wants me to

elaborate. I move my gaze to nothing in particular while the moment replays in my mind.

"That class was full of energetic kids, and she was the most chill of them all. That's probably why I didn't notice her until the end of our presentation. She was sitting in the back, and she looked like she was frustrated with the crossword activity her teacher had them doing."

I pause, remembering the now awkward connection: Shelby being Nova's teacher and the one that Joni saw me out with.

"I guess that's how you met Shelby, too, eh?" Joni asks, as if she read the shift in my energy.

"Yeaaah," I drag out, feeling low-key guilty, but then quickly say, "We didn't connect then, and I didn't. Nova was who she was until I sat down and helped her with the crossword puzzle. It wasn't really that hard, but I get it, things like that can be had for younger kids."

I can feel Joni's body react to a heavy breath she takes before she confides, "Nova has a learning disability. Dyslexia. For her, the letter sometimes gets jumbled in her mind, making reading and comprehension harder. The crossword puzzle probably didn't help, even if it was easy."

Thinking back to that time, it all made sense and I hum my understanding. It also made sense what she said about the signs and arrows at the museum. Something happens in my chest, like it expands, when I remember the fear and frustration that shaded Nova's face during both of the incidents.

I almost forgot that Joni is lying there until the tingle of her fingertips making circles on my chest pulls me out of my thoughts. Her voice cracks as she continues after a beat, "I'm protective of her because of that. It's new for both of us, and I've been wanting to make sure I understand it and she does too before adding anything else in our worlds to complicate it. Splitting her time between me and Malik is enough of a complication for an eight-year-old."

I can tell Joni is being vulnerable and speaking straight from her mind, or even her heart, because she spoke of Malik as if I were familiar. I quickly assume Malik is Nova's dad, the guy who was at the scene at the museum. I listen, taking it all in because this is the most Joni has ever let me in, and I'm eager to learn more.

When a stent of silence settles between us, I take the opportunity to pry a little more. "So, what happened with Nova's dad…Malik?"

She huffs and is quick to respond. "He cheated. A lot, and all the way up until I decided I had had enough of being the butt of the joke in the relationship we had. Nova was five when we split. Old enough to understand things were going to be different…complicated."

"I see," is all I offer as the picture of the guy comes to my mind again. He was a swole dude, but short, maybe a few inches shorter than me. He gave little man syndrome, and I can feel the scowl twitching in the corner of my mouth as I thought about how much of a fool he is to fumble Joni. Joni's reference to Malik and anything after being complicated echoes in my mind. I close my eyes as I decide to ask the next question. "Do you think I'm complicated?"

"No." Her answer is just as quick as her offering of the info on Malik and is accompanied by a soft chuckle. A hint of a question is hidden in the one word, too, which makes my stomach drop. "You're not complicated. We are, though."

My stomach cringes at her truth, but my mouth uncans, "We don't have to be."

I know, me saying this could make or break the rest of the getaway, but it's my truth, and honestly, I'm ready to lay everything on the table.

To my surprise, she softly admits, "You're right. I've been thinking about it a lot since…the museum."

Me too, I want to admit, but I let my mind run the show for a minute and keep my mouth shut.

"Nova looked so comfortable with you, and that took a load off of me…"

Her words trail as if there's a thought she isn't speaking. My eyes are open now, looking at the swirling ceiling fan above us as I wait for her to just say it. She doesn't, so I probe some more.

"Load like what, Joni?"

I feel her body tense, and her finger stops swirling before she reveals in a breath, "The load of having l-" she stops before her voice cracks again. "...love for someone and not being able to completely share it."

For a stretch in time, it feels like I had no breath to breathe, and there isn't a living beat in my chest, just silence, like my mind is making sure I heard what I heard and there wasn't anything to construe it. I want to be sure because I don't want to be a fool when I tell her:

"I got love for you, too, Joni." I pause, letting my words sink in. "I've loved you for a minute, but..." I snort. "...I guess you're right. We were complicated. But nothing's complicated to me right now. I know I want to be more than just somebody who stops by. I want to be in your life...and I know that includes Nova."

It's really quiet and still between us before Joni finally shifts. She lifts those spellbinding almond irises to me, sending this crazy warmth through my chest as she takes her hand to my face, softly running her fingertips over my stubble. "I want that, too."

"And this will be your table, Sir and Madame. Your Dining Concierge will be here momentarily."

The olive-complexion woman hostess swivels on her red-bottomed heels to Joni and me, fanning her hand over the table set for two. Her movement is swift and as stiff as her neck, and the taut bun sitting at the nape of her neck and my shoulders jump slightly from being taken aback. From my periphery, I can see Joni rear back her head, and I can only assume she's having the same experience as me. We look at each other, mimicking the same unsure wiggle of our eyebrows before I move to pull her chair out. When we take our seats, the woman turns to us again, her hands crossed at her lap and nose high.

"Is there anything I may do before I go?" she asks, her lips barely moving as she speaks with pretension thick in her syllables.

"Nah, we good," I answer, in my typical lingo. Joni kicks me under the table and bugs her eyes at me for it. I clear my throat and sit up more as I turn on my bourgeoisie. "We are doing exceptionally well at the moment, thank you."

The woman's eyes narrow slightly before she swivels again and stalks away. When she is a good way away, Joni and I look at each other and laugh.

"Mm, this place is too rich for me," Joni says lightheartedly. She opens the leather-bound menu and scans. "I feel like I need a trust fund to be eating here."

I open the menu, letting it lie flat on the table, and chuckle. I pretend to be engrossed in the menu, hoping my nervous uncertainty can't be detected.

I chose *Azul* almost blindly. I Googled "5-star southern brunch restaurants near the cove," and this restaurant popped up. The food looked good, and although pricey, I wanted to do something nice for Joni. I wanted to give her an experience and show her that I might be her "youngin," but I knew how to plan a date she could brag about to her girls. What I didn't quite pay attention to is that it's located outside of the Lovey's Bay Country Club on the outskirts of its golf course. It's a haven for old money and golf course junkies.

"I'm just playing." The softness of Joni's voice carries over the lull of voices and soft jazz in the background. I move my eyes up to her, quirking a half smile. "This is really nice, Tevin."

I sweep my eyes across the room, finally feeling confident enough to take in our surroundings. From outside of the white stucco building, you can't really tell what you're stepping into, but once you walk through the wooden, dark, arched doorway, you feel like you're walking into a members-only establishment. Simple yet luxe touches: waxed light oak wood floors against blinding cream-colored walls painted with embossed fancy waves. Gold accents elevate the restaurant, from the wall trim to the "gold" ware. Linen tables accompanied by rattan chairs tufted with turquoise blue cushions—I can admit I was hesitant to sit in them, even in my linen pants. My eyes land on its final destination, the golf course and Lovey's Bay in the distance. It's a dope view and an added touch to making the date memorable.

I shrug. "Yeah, it's cool, even if I have to open up the Dictionary written by T.I." I turn on my best T.I. impersonation and rattle off, "Scrumptious delectable delicacies…"

Joni's signature teetering laugh skates from her before she tries to stifle it with a hand to her mouth, and I snicker.

"Nah, don't hide that country ass laugh!"

"Shut up, Tevin!" she snorts and wheezes as she tries to hold it together.

I sit back in my chair, amused at the sounds coming from her. "No, you shut up before they throw us out of this good establishment."

Joni finds a way to muffle her laugh as our "dinner concierge" approaches our table. She appears less formal as the hostess and is possibly a college student. She introduces herself as Thierry and gives a few suggestions from the menu.

"Mm, I think the Duck Fat Waffle and Hot Honey Chicken thighs sound good. I'll take that, and could I order the Azul 75?"

Thierry taps on her tablet and nods pleasantly. "Absolutely. And for you, sir?"

"Uh, let me get that Smoked gouda grits. Can you

throw some shrimp on it?" I ask, looking up from the menu.

She meets my inquiry with a quick nod. "Absolutely. And what drink would you like to indulge in with your meal?"

"Let me get that Carolina Gold. Premium bourbon."

With a final nod, Thierry takes our menus and prances off. Only a few minutes and small talk between Joni and me occupy the time before Thierry comes back with our drinks. Joni's drink, the Azul 75, resembles a French 75, but with a twist: it's poured into a champagne flute and features a lavender color instead of the typical pale yellow. My drink looks like a classic Bourbon, but when I sip, I'm invigorated by the spice of ginger liqueur and the sweetness of peach juice.

"Whew this joint smooth," I muse, taking a more languid sip.

Joni has nearly finished her glass and agrees, "Mine is delicious, too."

I scoff, deciding to tease Joni. "I see Big Mama. You took that down like a real G."

She huffs another boyant laugh just as a collaboration of thunderous laughter overpowers hers. There's a door behind Joni, providing an entrance from the golf course where a group of men walked through. They were brothas but dressed like squares, all dressed in polos and tight ass khaki shorts. As they rounded past our table, they acknowledged Joni and me with nods, with one familiar-looking S-Curl slowing and then stopping.

"Joni?"

Joni stiffens and her eyes widen when she recognizes the person addressing her. "Uh, Avery."

Joni's words come out choppy, evident in her surprise at seeing the guy I remembered seeing her with at the movies. She moves her eyes to me and then back to him nervously, making me wonder what there was to be nervous about. She stands and gives him the hug he beckons for. My jaw tenses as I watch him wrap his arms around her nearly bare waistline. For a moment, I regretted giving her the thumbs-up on the summer dress. I love it on her; it mimics a two-piece with a halter-like top that hugs her perfect, teardrop breasts. It attaches to the flowing skirt by strings that crisscross over her midsection. It's sexy as hell, but with this guy ogling her in it, I want to pull the linen off our table and wrap her in it.

The square pulls back from the two-second-too-long hug. "I hope my flowers find you well. I haven't heard from you."

Flowers? When did he send her flowers?

Joni's goofy laugh is no longer there, but has been replaced by a wispy, nervous one as she moves her eyes to me again and steps back from Avery to sit back in her seat. "Yeah. They did, umm, thank you. Let me introduce you to…my man. Tevin."

My puzzled scowl lifts with my eyebrows when I hear her introduction. I kiss my teeth smugly as I stand, extending a hand. Ol' boy looks shocked and low-key disappointed but accepts my dap. He gives me a once-over that I didn't want to let slide, but for the sake of not wanting to be a stereotype, I let it slide. My mind doesn't let it go, though, pondering how close the two of them had gotten, and when was the last time she received flowers from this dude?

He chuckles. "Like, little Tevin Campbell."

I catch Joni wincing as I drop a dry laugh. "Something like that, I'll take it. He did have the ability to steal your girl…" I huff another laugh watching Avery's eyes shift and jaw tick. "…you know with his voice."

Avery slips his hand from mine and dryly responds, "Yeah. Right." He turns back to Joni, making the quick exit I had hoped for. "It was good seeing you, Joni. Perhaps we'll talk again."

Joni drops a mousy, "Yeah," before waving quickly and putting her glass to her lips, finishing the few drops left. A heavy silence settles between us, with Joni clearly trying to figure out what to say. I help her.

"So, uh, your man, huh? Was that just to get him to buzz off?"

She looks at me as if to ask me about my audacity,

but then her eyes soften. "No, I didn't say it as a way to get him to leave. It's the truth." She ticks her arched brow up. "You're my man, right?"

I feel the crease in my forehead still settled deep from the interaction with the brotha from Soul Glo as I stared her down, affirming, "No doubt about it, baby."

"We only went out once, Tevin, and it was the day I saw *you* with Nova's teacher," Joni confesses. I can hear the playful irritation in her voice, but I keep my eyes on the road. "I could be asking you twenty-one questions about Shelby, you know?"

"You could, but you ain't. It's about you and Slick Back Jack right now," I say with all seriousness behind my shameless dig. "So, about these flowers. He still sending you flowers?"

"Tevin…"

I continue to listen to Joni explain how she met Avery and what did and did not happen while we drive the few minutes from Azul back to our home away from home. After Avery left our table, we enjoyed our meal, but my mind still reeled over his presence, the way he looked and touched, and that wack ass dig he made to me. I know, I got the prize. I have the woman by way of her claim of me in front of him. Still, my blood bubbled at the faded vision of the whole scene floating through my head.

"Tevin, let's not spend our last night talking about Avery. Please?" Joni's request came through a hopeful sigh after we entered the house. She leads the way and only pauses with her request as she reaches the deck doors.

I fold my arms across my chest, taking a hand to my stubbled chin, and peruse her fine ass. I can see her annoyance shading her face while she tries to keep her gaze soft. She wets her plump bottom lip as she waits for my response. The simple gesture made my groin tight. "We're not."

She breathes, "Thank you," and then turns, pushing the doors open. As she walks out, I can't help but notice the jiggle of her ass beneath her dress. The allure of a panty-less ass under a summer dress had my animal instincts settling in. I want to pounce on her, my prey, like I am Mufasa, but at the same time make an example out of Avery like Scar. I swagger through the door behind Joni with a mix of both intentions.

Joni is propped between a corner of the deck with a view of the bay, with her back to me when I approach. A minuscule breeze wafts a mix of the salt air and her coconut scent, turning out to be a combination that only heightens my prowl. I close into Joni, immediately feeling the heat of her body elevate mine as I take place behind her, placing a hand on either side of her. I can feel her body relax against me, my growing manhood nestling between her cheeks.

"That shit ol' boy pulled made my skin crawl," I grumble into her ear. I feel her tense, but move too quickly to alleviate, running my fingertips up the length of her arm as she starts to groan my name. It tapers off when I kiss the space between her jawline and ear. "But you claiming me as your man made me heavy for you. Can you feel it?"

A breathy moan floats with the breeze from Joni as she melts into my touch again. She angles her head towards me with each kiss trailing across her jawline. When I get to her gaping mouth, I whisper my affirmation.

"You're mine. All mine now. You feel me?" I rasp, letting the connotation of my words be taken and felt at the same time. I linger my lips over hers, listening and feeling her shallow breath while pressing my erection into her. The material of her dress caves and acts like a barrier between me and the split of her bubble ass. That shit aggravates the irritation and desire that fight for dominance.

In a whimper, she replies, "Mm-hmm," pushing into me and chasing my lips with her tongue. I give her mouth, letting my tongue dance teasingly with hers before breaking the kiss.

Nibbling on her ear, I groan, "I don't think you feel me yet."

Joni has this sexy ass laugh she does when she's feeling naughty. It's low, air, and short, and the sound of it as she taunts, "Make me feel it then, Tevin," makes the tip of my dick wet.

I don't waste time. I don't even give a damn that it's broad daylight in the middle of the day. She wants to feel it, and I want to ruin her for the next—no, for the man who will never get a chance with her. I'm the one and done. I'm the captain.

I kiss down the side of her neck until I meet the nape of her neck while unfastening my belt and pants. My pants fall open, but hang on my hips. It's enough for me to fist my rock-hard length as it plops out of my briefs. I bunch a handful of her dress and lift it, just enough to dip low and rock my head against her opening. Her cream coats my length as I sink into her, almost simultaneously to the crash of the waves hitting the beach.

"Ooh, shit…" she moans and arches her back up to me as I reach her depth. I pull out halfway and rock back in, slowly stroking her as I wrap an arm around her waist and move my free hand up the center of her chest until my hand is wrapped around her neck.

I nip at her ear again, finding pleasure in her shallow pants. "You feel me yet?"

She doesn't say anything; instead, she lets out a muted, open-mouthed moan.

I pull out slowly but only halfway and thrust into her with force. I can tell it's pleasurable for her by the way her walls clench around my dick and the sink of her teeth into her lip. Her face contorts, displaying the pleasure she's trying to control. I didn't want controlled pleasure after coming face-to-face with the man who failed at taking my place.

I drag my dick out and then pound.

She bites harder.

Drag and pound.

She whimpers.

Drag and pound.

She cries out, breathily, "Fuck me, Tevin."

Her words come out in between a beg and a command. I give her what she wants. I pound relentlessly into her while holding her up to me. When I thrust into her next, I feel her wetness gush down my thigh. I have to bite down on my lip to keep from bussing, but it doesn't stop me from thrusting again.

"The next time he sends you flowers, throw them shits away," I growl between my teeth, feeling the veins in my dick jumping.

"Okay…okay.." She whimpers through another set of thrusts.

I grunt and pinch my eyes shut, nearly at my wits'

end as I thrust into her again. She felt so fucking good. She sounds so fucking good. When I open my eyes, I see an elderly man stepping out on his deck, alerting me to just how close in proximity we were to our weekend neighbor. He wasn't up on us to know what we were doing, but close enough that if he squinted his aged eyes a bit, he could tell. I still, but don't pull out.

"Baby, fix your face," I murmur into Joni's ear. I feel her tense against me when she realizes we have a visitor. With ease, I wrap my arms around her waist, still nestled into her spasming pussy. The sensation has me sipping in a slow breath before I exhale instructions, my eyes still trained on the man who has now noticed us. "Just smile and wave."

"Tevin, what…the..fuck…" she titters.

Her voice is barely audible over the crashing waves, but I catch it. Giving her a reassuring squeeze, I whisper, "Smile, baby," before I clear my throat and greet the unaware man with a head nod.

The man looks to be in his late sixties, with a neatly trimmed salt and pepper mustache and a low haircut that stands out against his reddish brown complexion. He's dressed in a nautical button-up shirt and shorts, and I hoped that meant he wouldn't be on his deck much longer and would be heading down his steps towards the beach. Being sunken in Joni's abyss was a tortured plea-sure. I wasn't sure I would make it through much longer.

I'm forced to, however, because the man decides to start a fucking conversation. I begin to make little rocks into her to alleviate the sensation to buss.

"Beautiful day, isn't it?" he asks, planting himself firmly on his deck. He places his arms on his hips like he's setting up to begin a long conversation. I can feel Joni's stomach filling and emptying in shaky intervals, clear that she's on the brink of her climax just like me. The man looks from me to Joni, still oblivious of my mini pumps into Joni's quivering pussy. A chill runs through me in reaction to her pussy pulse, and I accidentally push deeper into her.

"Y-yes!" Joni squeals in a way that makes the man jump and look between us awkwardly this time before he frowns in confusion and walks back into his home. The moment I hear the faint click of his door securing, I go to town on that pussy.

"Tevin…" Joni whimpers her beg. At first, her hands are placed on top of mine, wrapped around her waist, but they fall to the edge of the deck as she starts unraveling. She arches her back further as she leans, tooting that pretty ass up. I envision the ripples her ass is making under the skirt, disappointed I couldn't watch without the cover of the peach material. The mental visual is enough to bring forth the fireworks as I grab hold of her waist for the last round of unabated thrusts.

"Mm-hmm, that's my name, baby. The only name you gon' speak again….gahdamn…!"

All of a sudden, the trumpets that start Kanye West's "All of the Lights" blare in my head, and all I see is lights and stars and confetti on the back of my eyelids. I explode, and Joni's finale follows behind, echoing through the air. I'm sure as hell it caused a few people to stop and look around to determine the threat. The only threat they'll find is the undoing of my sanity if I ever let Joni get away.

Spent, I pull out of Joni, our breaths struggling for unison. Lazily shimmying her dress down, she turns and slumps her back against the wooden banister and stares at me with blissful bewilderment clouding her eyes. "What…what are you trying to do to me?"

Roaming my hands around her hips to cup her ass, I give her a firm squeeze and snicker. "Don't worry about it. It's already done."

JONI

"You know I love my girl, Nina, but I'm type irked that she has us going on a Bridal Boat Ride for her bachelorette."

"Why? And tilt your head down."

I tilt my head down, my chin hitting my chest, and wait for a moment, letting Tevin start the lineup of my nape before I begin my rant again. "Tevin, you know why…the killer seagulls."

The buzz of the clippers abruptly turns off before Tevin's audacious laugh fills the bathroom. I whip my head up to look at him in the vanity mirror. He meets my gaze as his laugh simmers into a chuckle, a glimmer of sympathy in his eyes. "Babe, I don't think you're going to have to worry about seagulls on a night cruise."

Tevin leans in and kisses my neck, his way of telling me to lower my head again so he can finish lining me up. I do, but continue with a ramble of facts as the clippers start again. "Well, according to Nova, seagulls do come out at night if there's artificial lighting or food around. Both are gonna be on that boat."

I hear his chortle before he asks, "Wait, when did Nova tell you this fact? I haven't heard this one before."

I shrug. "Mm, a couple of days ago, during our weekly check-in. I told her about the bridal shower and you know my Supanova…"

"…always with a fact," Tevin finishes for me, but then jokes, "I'm gonna need you two to stop obsessing over the one animal that's highly unlikely to attack."

"Whatever you say," I sing-song. "Don't say anything if you all get pulled from the bachelor party because we are getting eaten by my killer seagulls."

The vibration of the hair clippers is replaced with more kisses from Tevin, one in the center of my neck that's trailed by light pecks to the crook of my neck. His kisses always melt on my skin like snow falling to the ground, and make me feel just as serene as the snow visual. I close my eyes and stretch my neck to the right to indulge his affections, but he stops, and I hear him pad away. I peel one eye open to the mirror, confirming the empty space behind me, and then twist my hips to the door frame leading to my room, finding Tevin getting comfortable on my bed on his back, his head slightly hanging off the edge as he lies horizontally.

He moves his eyes to me and nods his head to the side, beckoning me. "Come here. Let me eat that worry away."

An unsuspecting chortle escapes me just as a wave of heat floats through my body, landing right into my center. Tevin doesn't flinch. His face shows he's earnest about making me his morning meal. I'm not one to deny him, even if he disguises his want for me in wanting to release my worries. I saunter over, tasting my lips at the thought of him tasting me, and straddle his face. The briskness of the air as he pushes my satin robe over my ass sends an anticipatory chill through me, and when he lowers me onto his face, the warmth of his breath has my kitty purring for what's to come.

"Fuck, Tevin…" I moan at the intoxicating sensation of the heat of his mouth and the slow, wet drag of his tongue against my already swollen bud.

The ride of Tevin's tongue is one amusement I would never pass up, and one he hasn't revoked my ticket to yet. In fact, since our getaway, "Tevin's Playhouse" has been open nearly every day, providing me the thrill of his tongue and his always-in-salute erection, just like old times. The way we've been at it, I'm surprised my kitty hasn't packed her bags and left, but I guess the desire to want something all the time is what comes with being in love, right?

That's what it's like now. I want Tevin all the time, but this isn't necessarily a new thing. I've always wanted him and his skills—whether it's his penis or his mouth; all of him always provided me with the fun and thrill of a good time. Now, however, it's not just fun and thrill. There's love wrapped all in every dip…and drop…and swirl…

"I feel like cayenne pepper!" I breathe the Jill Scott line floating through my head aloud.

I did feel like the smoldering pepper, being masterfully devoured by Tevin. I roll my hips forward and, knowing exactly what I want, he latches onto my pearl and rhythmically taps his tongue. Back arched and fingers clawing at the sheet underneath him, my legs shake at the spikes of pleasure jolting through my body.

"Mm-hmm, cum all in my mouth," he groans. Chasing after my release, Tevin hooks his arms around my thighs, securing my pussy over his mouth. He slurps, and I proceed to smother him with my juices. His satisfied moans roll another wave through my body, and I fall forward, coming face to face with his rock-hard sidekick.

After a job well done, he deserves a job only my mouth can properly perform.

"Lift up for me, baby," I purr, tapping the side of his hip.

Tevin grunts his amusement and understanding and lifts, just enough for me to roll his briefs down and be greeted by the wobble of his immaculate, curved dick. My mouth waters at the sight of its stature, the protruding veins… its girth. I rim the inner edge of my lip and open up wide, inviting him into my mouth.

"Fuck."

The single word falls from Tevin's lips through a breath as my mouth slides down half of his shaft before I have to work my way back up and ready my mouth to take in more of him. With slow bobs, I inch more and more of him into my mouth, my saliva thickening and spilling over his length. He's so big that my cheeks ache as I try to swallow him whole. I love that for me. When his tip hits the back of my throat, I gag and moan, which sets off a breathless moan from Tevin.

My oral pleasure encourages him to go another round on me, and my God, if round two isn't heaven in a sinful moment. My girl has no idea what to do—spasm, clench, sputter—she does it all, and I moan and suck my way through it.

Faster.

Deeper.

Bang! Bang! Bang!

Slurping.

Gagging.

Bang! Bang! Bang!

. . .

"Ugh…fuck!" I groan, or maybe moan.

The following noise that comes from me is definitely a groan, because who the hell is at my door? I try to lift from Tevin, but he puts a death grip on my ass and begins to…

"Mmmm…Tevin…!" I whimper to the vibration of his hum. "I gotta…I gotta..."

"Cum for me." His mumbled command, the sensation of his tongue, the urgency to reach my glory….I unravel —hard and loud. The smack to my ass jolts a mini tremor through my body, all while the mystery person still knocks on my door. Tevin snickers, "You can go get the door now."

If it weren't for the person at my door, I probably would stay right here and finish him like a Mortal Kombat fighter whose secret weapon is a mean deep throat. Instead, I scoot to the edge of the bed, adjust the belt of my robe, and walk away on numb, wobbly legs, only glancing over my shoulder at him to shoot a narrowed eye. I had no words. He sucked them out of me.

Only when I opened the door did my brain remember how to configure letters into words.

"Nova..Malik…"

Nova and Malik meet my wide, surprised eyes with

expressions of their own. Nova wears a big, cheesy smile as she wraps her arms around my waist while Malik looks at me, perplexed. I catch him do a glance over me, and I quickly pull my robe's lapel a little tighter over myself, brushing over my hard nipples. I curse myself internally for still wearing the remnants of the effect of Tevin.

"I told you I was bringing Nova back today…" Malik says, almost quizzical.

I chuckle, trying to fade away my surprise. "Yeah, but you didn't say when. You two are never here this early."

It's a Sunday, yes, the usual day that Malik would bring Nova home, but when I look over my left shoulder to the clock on the kitchen wall, it reads nearly eleven in the morning. Nova typically comes home in the late afternoon…which is why Tevin and I shared a lazy, free-spirited morning. I didn't have a problem with Tevin being here when Nova came home, but a heads up would've been nice so that I wouldn't run the risk of Nova stumbling into this: me in a sexual afterglow with Tevin half naked—

I whip my head to the right towards the door of my room, remembering I wobbled to the front door without securing my door. When I look, I sigh in relief, seeing that the door is closed with a slight crack. That's when my annoyance kicks in.

"Malik, you could've called or text…something," I fuss, tapping Nova on the back, giving her a subtle nudge to head to her room. When she takes off, I fold my arms over my chest. "That's what you've been doing."

Malik chuckles as he runs his tongue over his teeth. "My bad, J. We went to breakfast on this side of town, and Nova was ready to see her mom…" His words trail as he lustfully trails his eyes down my frame again. I shifted in my stance, getting the ick from his ogle. "You lookin' good, Baby Mama."

I roll my eyes hard, ready to say something slick when I feel a presence behind me. The glare that sets in Malik's eyes as he lifts them above me confirms what I already knew. Tevin placed his right hand on the door seal and leaned down to kiss my cheek, solidifying it.

"Everything good, babe?"

I look over my shoulder and up to Tevin. He's clothed now in his usual white shirt and company shorts. The way he made his way over the wooden floors without me hearing him told me he is barefoot and comfortable. His six-feet-something frame always made me feel smaller than I already am, but his energy now, as he stands so close to me that I can feel the heat of his glare at Malik, made me feel like a chihuahua to a big dog. My "Yeah" staggers out as he reaches over me and extends his hand to Malik.

"What up, I'm Tevin. You must be…Malik?"

I move my eyes to Malik, my mouth slightly parted and unsure if I should say anything. He hesitates as he tries to size Tevin up, but he stops as he realizes how much more he has to look up to him, clearly feeling his little man syndrome setting in. With reluctance, he takes Tevin's hand for an unenthused dap.

"Yeah, nice to meet you…" He gruffs and then looks to me, dropping his hand from Tevin's. "I didn't know you had company."

"Tevin!"

"Supanova!"

Nova's very enthusiastic voice and then her sneakers hitting the floor at record speed are heard before I can turn around. She snaps her little body to his side before he scoops her up. My heart flutters, and I feel my face heating with a blush until I realize Malik is still standing there. For a second, I tense up, but then the inkling to give a fuck fades as I return to my stance to face him. I cock my head to the side.

"You've known I had company if you had called, but now you know."

I unfold an arm and motion for him to roll Nova's suitcase to me. Tevin and Nova can be heard catching up behind me. Malik's beady eyes keep trying to stretch past me to the two. I clear my throat and swerve my head in his view, beckoning for the suitcase again. Again, despite the reluctance, he does so.

"Thanks," I sing, clutching the handle of the suitcase and rolling it over the threshold. "See you next week? Oh, and make sure you call first."

I don't wait for him to say anything before I close the door.

25

JONI

The summer went by entirely too fast. With just a week before the first day of school, Nova and I are weaving through the busy shopping park, Shoppes at Palm Cove.

I didn't expect any less of a crowd. It's a clear, sunny Friday in August, and the temperature still sits in the low eighties even with it nearing the six o'clock hour. With the combination of it being the beginning of an expected clear weekend and back-to-school shopping in full effect, everybody from teenagers and families to people lounging in the small park in the middle of the shopping center with their furry friends is out. Despite the busyness, we are making strides in our shopping, but Nova says one thing that tells me our time is ticking.

"Mommy, I'm hungry."

Nova didn't just say this; she whined her complaint, and when I looked down at her as we walked out of The Children's Spot, she looked at me with pleading eyes and an undeniable pout. To add to the drama, she trudges along as if she is truly famished, her Converse soles scraping and then clunking against the concrete.

I run my hand over the tail of her curly ponytail. "We're almost done, boops. We just have to get your school shoes, and then we can go eat."

A small whimper mixes in with her sigh as she pokes her lip further as she asks, "Promise?"

"Promise."

The corner of my mouth curves into a half smile, coercing a hopeful one from Nova, and we forge forward to our last stop, hand in hand. Some time during our walk, I hear a muffled ding from my phone.

Tevin: You swing those hips any harder, you're gonna hurt somebody.

I stop dead in my tracks, yo-yoing Nova back to me, and frown at my phone. I crane my head to the left and right, but it's Nova who sees him first, yanking from my grip on her hand and running behind me. When I swing around to scold her for running off, my fixed mouth relaxes as I bite away a blush.

"Mr. Tevin!" Nova squeals as Tevin scoops her up with one arm. With the other, he restrained a leash holding Frenchie, his French bulldog. I hadn't seen Frenchie since I stopped going to Tevin's house when his volunteer moved in.

"Look out! It's a shooting star!"

Tevin's voice carries through the air as he lifts Nova in the air, releasing her from his arms only for a few seconds before she comes back down into his grasp. Nova's screech causes a few bystanders to look on amused. As for me, I look on with heavy, adoring eyes. The image of him before me, still dressed in his navy blue fire department collared shirt and matching work pants and shoes, holding my little girl, makes goosebumps prickle up the back of my neck and my heart swell—total, utter turn on. I simper for a moment and wonder to myself:

Why did you wait so long?

The thought consumes me with dread like every other time I think it, and that's happened more than once over the last few weeks. Since Nova's return home, Tevin's been spending more time around—before dark. It only made sense. Nova knew who he was without giving her adult details. She knew he was "mommy's friend" and seemed to take to it fine, and so was I. If Nova is adjusting to Tevin's presence well, so am I more and more, and truthfully, if I wade past my previous hesitation of this reality, it's exactly what I hoped for. I fought hard to keep my two lives apart, but deep down, I wanted to have them merge. Tevin has meant more to me than just a good deliverer of dick for a long time. I just didn't know if this was just all fun or something that could be solid. From the looks of how my two favorite people take to each other, it's all solid.

"What are you doing here?" I coo after pulling away from Tevin's embrace. He doesn't let me go far with his arms still snug around my waist. I cut my eyes to the right, making a quick observation of Nova's whereabouts. I see her playing with Frenchie, not too far from us, in the greenery. She giggles and jerks her head back as Frenchie tries to lick her face.

He hums, "Mmm. I got out of training with the crew a little early and thought I'd give Frenchie some new scenery."

I twist my mouth, not buying his excuse at all. "So you drive 15 minutes across town to take Frenchie on a five-minute walk here, huh?"

"Yeah," he quips before chuckling and pecking my lips. "…and I thought I'd try to catch up with you and Nova. Is that a problem?"

A small, unrecognizable voice comes from me as I admit, "No," and fall into his embrace again. I didn't know who I was turning into, talking in baby voices and blushing every five minutes. Oh, who was I kidding? I am turning into a woman deep in love—and basking in it aloud.

"C'mon, Nova baby. We're here."

I don't know why I am still rushing, but I am, damn near jumping out of my sedan and slamming my door. It was the rushed energy that bubbled in me from the moment I left work. It was four-thirty, the start of rush hour, and I had to make it to Nina's house to pick up Nova. She'd spent the day with Nina, helping her with Aidan and curating keepsakes Nina insisted on doing herself for the Bridal Shower Cruise this weekend. That was a thirty-minute drive, thanks to the bumper-to-bumper traffic, and then I had to make it back into town in enough time to grab Nova a bite to eat and get to Back to School Night on time, all still during the after-work traffic.

I've never understood why schools start Back to School Night at six, knowing most of us who work are flying around like bats out of hell trying to get there, me being one of the number of bats flying out of hell. Yet, I make it, with five minutes to spare. I pause to breathe when Nova is out of the car and standing beside me with a mouthful of nuggets.

"I'm sorry for the rush, baby," I breathe, feeling the tension in my body slowly ease away. The sight of her swollen cheeks as she takes big, rolling chews makes me giggle empathetically.

All Nova offers me is a shrug as she continues to munch and swallow. I place a hand on her back and do a quick glance over her, ensuring her hair is intact and her floral dress clings to her appropriately, before I give her a light tap, signaling for her to start moving with me. We take maybe five steps before we are halted by Malik blocking our path to the school entrance.

"Heyy, Daddy's girls!"

Ew.

My face contorts at his awkward and unusual greeting. He looks like he just got off work, too, dressed in a fitted black button-up and grey slacks. He stretches his arms out and begins to swagger towards us. By his second step, I have stepped out of his grasp, causing his movements to stutter slightly before he engulfs Nova in his embrace.

Malik looks up at me as Nova plants a kiss on his cheek and chuckles, "No group hugs?"

"We don't do that," I quip, my voice rising an octave. I lift my eyes and a freshly arched brow at him as he stands upright, while the corner of my lip curls up, making my disgust evident. My look doesn't faze him because he keeps yapping while he and Nova stay on my heels as I walk towards the entrance.

"We should. We're still family, you know?"

I stop just shy of the door, craning my neck as I look back at him, confused as hell at this "family" talk. I choose not to even entertain it and proceed to swing the metal door open and guide Nova in first before I follow behind her. I don't hold the door open for Malik either, and hear his heavy body thud against the door as he tries to catch it.

Malik has been on one since the day he met Tevin. All of a sudden, he wants to text me randomly and not talk about Nova. He'll text and want to have small talk as if that was something we normally did. Again, we don't do that. We never had, and I had no plans to do that. All I want is to co-parent our child cordially and leave the boundary-pushing pleasantries he wants to incorporate out of the equation because none of this felt friendly…at all.

But it's back-to-school night, and he is my co-parent, and despite the bullshit, I must follow my own words and be cordial. A groan rumbles in my throat as I fight with myself for being so mature. However, my maturity is tested two seconds later when I see two familiar people being *too familiar*.

"Oh my God, Tevin, you are so funny!" Shelby, Nova's bombshell of a teacher, lilts. Her voice is a babyish soprano, and her laugh floats like a happy little hummingbird at whatever Tevin must've said.

What the hell is so funny?

It all felt and sounded familiar. I talk and flirt with Tevin like this. I can feel my pressure rising, and the chatter in the hallway starts to blur under the ringing of my ears. I force a cleansing breath, but it doesn't do much to cleanse the irk in my bones.

My eyes narrow as they bounce to Tevin, cheesin' like a rapper with a new set of veneers. Straight ahead of me, he stands behind a table in front of a case of school awards. Hanging from the edge of the table is a sign that reads "Start the School Year Off Safe- Lovey's Bay Fire Department." Seeing the sign tells my logical brain that Tevin's here on duty, and so does seeing some of his volunteer crew I've seen before…but he didn't tell me he would be here. Not during his good morning text. Not even when I talked to him during lunch. Not a single word.

Did Shelby know?

I can't front, even with the fact that Tevin will most likely end his night at my place, the small detail of him being at Back to School night going without being said, and seeing the woman he had a short stint of a romance with, rattles my nerves. It doesn't help that my ratchet right side of my brain starts shooting steam and firing off as Shelby hooks her arm into Tevins and runs her French tip acrylics down his arm.

"Oh, hell no…" I say under my breath. The war between my left and right sides of my brain is being fought to no end right now. I know I am probably overreacting, but am I? I've seen this scenario play out before, and that was with Malik's eye-wandering self. I'm not sure when I let my right brain win, but I did. With no clear plans or intention, I let the clack of my heels lead the way ahead.

Fuck it.

The number of times I checked my watch and the double doors in front of me is absurd. Every time I hear the faint whine of the hinges of the heavy door or the clank of the door securing, I turn into a bobble head, searching for who I expect to walk through the door: Joni and Nova.

I didn't tell Joni I'd be at Back to School Night with the V-Squad, manning the Fire Department's display table to welcome the families back to school, as well as be a visual reminder of fire safety. I like the way they respond when I surprise them, so I let my ego talk me into staying quiet, although it was hard as well. Every time she asked me what my plans were for this evening, I had to remember the lie I told her about studying for a few hours for my first exam in my Fire Science class. I cringe thinking about lying to her, but it isn't a complete lie. I did do a little studying earlier, just not at the time I told her. It's just a little white lie for the sake of seeing their faces light up when they walk through the doors and see me front and center.

"Damn, Tev, you're watching the door like the feds are about to come through." I peel my gaze from the door and look to Jace. He's standing to the right of me, chuckling at his joke. I can't help but chuckle. It was clever.

"Nah, I'm looking for Joni, but her nosy ass could work for the Feds though."

Jace snorts and shakes his head, his loose locs swaying with each move. "You wild. Her kid goes here?"

"Yep," I answer, nodding my head like a proud dad. I look back towards the door at the sound of a little laughing. Nope, it wasn't Nova. "I didn't tell them I'd be here. I wanted to surprise them."

"Damn, look at you sounding like a stepdad and shit. That's big dawg status."

Hearing the vulgar word, I whip my head to him, pinning him with a glare underneath the furrow of my brows. I shake my hand at him with each word, "We're at a family-friendly function. Chill on vulgarness."

Jace's eyebrows lift apologetically as he winces. He opens his mouth for what I assume is to apologize, but then he stops and moves his eyes past me. My chest lurches, thinking Joni and Nova must've finally made it. My heart gets stuck in my throat when I turn around and see Shelby strutting closer, the sway of her hips dripping with flirtatious intent.

"Well, well, look who the kitty dragged in…"

What would have been an insult in any other case, Shelby says, this is full of sensual innuendo. The way she props her round hip in the stonewash denim jeans she wears against the Fire Department display table and supports herself with her arm, intentionally poking her full breast further out through her soft, sheer button-down top, reinforces it, too.

"Shelby…hey…" I breathe, a nervous smile playing peekaboo in the corner of my mouth.

I hadn't seen her since I put her in a rideshare so that I could chase Joni down. I feel like any other woman would be ready to slap the taste out of my mouth after that, but not Shelby. She sits there with lustful eyes and a smirk.

"It's been so long since I've seen you," she coos. "How you been?"

She leans to place a hand on my arm, and smoothly, I cross them. The last thing I need is for Joni to walk in and think something's going on. We are on too good of terms for me to let someone in my past ruin it with her flirtation.

I keep an even and polite tone when I answer, "I've been good. Did you enjoy your summer?"

Shelby tilts her head back and lets out a sigh that almost sounds inappropriate for an elementary school setting. She tilts her head up and groans, "Oh, how the summer has come and gone too quickly!"

"Gone like wigs on a windy day," I joke, chuckling lightly. As for Shelby, she howls and doubles over, slapping her knee at my witty remark. She laughs so hard she nearly topples over, but catches herself by releasing her hip from its seated position. I catch her by the elbow for reassurance.

"Oh, My God! Tevin, you're so funny!" she guffaws.

I'm still geeking over her exasperated laugh when I realize she's looped her arm into mine and is now running her fingers down my bicep. Her touch does nothing for me, not even raise a fine hair on my arm, and immediately I think about Joni and what this would look like if she walked up on it.

Almost immediately after this thought, I hear Jace behind me, clearing his throat and mumbling, "Ahem, your girl is on the way."

When I look up, there's Joni, strutting with smoke coming from her heels and fire dancing in her eyes. Her expression stays muted, but before she stops in front of the table, I can feel the wrath within the misunderstood interaction.

Fuck.

"Joni, babe.." I race out. I take two steps away from Shelby while unconsciously nudging Shelby off my arm. I hear Shelby's light scoff, and I glance at her with apologetic eyes before I give my baby all of my attention. Joni catches the moment and raises a stiff eyebrow, questioning my audacity. I see her take a stiff breath before she tries to transform her scowl into something lighter. It doesn't work.

"Miss Shelby. Tevin," she greets in a sweet yet damn near eerie cadence. "Well, I haven't seen this picture since the movies."

"We're not together," I blurt out, taking another step to my right and bumping into Jace. Y'all remember that meme that came about when the two guys were battle rapping and the one guy twists his mouth like he didn't believe a word ol' boy was saying? That's the face Jace makes as he steps from the table, also known as Hell's Kitchen right now. I look to Joni, pleading with my eyes as I work to reaffirm my statement, "She just walked up to the table that *my crew and I* are working..."

"I see. This is the first time hearing you'd here..." Joni looks down at the table and scoffs lightly as she taps a finger on a brochure. She moves her eyes up to me. "I'm surprised because you had every opportunity when you were laid up with me last night..."

Joni slides her eyes to Shelby. They read, "Bitch, do you get the point?" while her smile showed pleasantries.

My baby is jealous. For no reason, though.

That shit turned me the fuck on.

"Oh…Honey, he ain't even worth it…"

My head cocks to Shelby's eye-roll and scoff to Joni, low-key offended, but the way Joni shifts in her stance, Shelby will be the culprit of her offense if I don't cool things off. I step around Shelby and the table, ready to brace Joni from taking another step, when my steps falter as Joni's lump-head ass baby daddy comes over, bracing to put his arm around Joni's shoulder.

"You good, J-Bird?"

J-Bird?

"Man, if you don't flap your ass away from my lady," I roast, flicking his arm away before it lands.

Joni jumps at the bold move and gasps, "Tevin!"

I see Jace stepping into my periphery, reminding me, "Uhh..Capo…family friend…vulgarity?"

I shoot him a dagger side eye while Malik starts to bark again, "Aye, kid. Joni is always gonna be family, and I'm gonna make sure my family good, ya feel me?"

"Malik…" Joni scoffs again, this time at Malik, stepping away and putting a hand up. "Don't even…we aren't even like that. You are baby daddy and that's it."

"*That's it,*" I reinforce, probably with a little too much bass in my voice, because a few parents look on to the scene, and then I see Nova, stepping to her mother's side with confusion dancing in her eyes as she looks to the three of us. My stomach hollows, and I see the moment Joni turns cold with guilt.

"This feels weird," Nova delivers in only a way she can. It's monotone in voice, but full of clear observation of what's happening right now. Her eyes are rounded behind her glasses, not in fear, but intrigue. Joni pulls her close to her hip and bends to plant frantic kisses on her head.

"Oh, no, Nova. Everything fine. Just fine. Come on, let's go meet your new teacher."

Joni whisks her away without more than a second glance at me, and my heart thudded, feeling the invisible door shutting as she departs with Malik trailing behind her and Nova. I'm left there in the middle of the hallway, kids and parents moving around me. Shelby, at some point, tiptoes away like a thief in the night while Joni turns into a dot in the sea of people as she walks further down the hallway.

I gotta fix this shit tonight, I think to myself, not realizing that she would be avoiding me the rest of the evening.

27

TEVIN

"I'm making a mental note not to let Joss suggest the spot for a bachelor party again," I mumble, loud enough for our crew surrounding me to hear as we walk through the double doors of a lounge.

A lounge. Not a strip club. Not even a music-blaring dance club.

When planning Denzel's bachelor party, Joss mentioned a members-only social club in Regency, called The Bank. She stated it was the perfect spot for her bachelor party because of the atmosphere and the exclusivity. It's exclusive, alright; we were being escorted through the main room by security, but the place didn't look like there was a need for all of the fanfare or protection. No one seems like they would cause trouble in here. Most are suited and booted, looking as though they were discussing business deals from the tables or leather-bound sectionals they were seated in. The few women I see are scattered amongst them, either seated primly and properly at the bar or used as pawn pieces by some of the men. Other than them, hostesses weave through the crowd, dressed in what looks like a uniform: sexy black midi-dresses, black sheer stockings, and matching stilettos. It wasn't giving "Best Bachelor Party of the Year" vibes.

I make quick glances across the crew. Deacon and Jace look like they are thinking the same thing, while Denzel, the ever-so "make the best out of everything" one in our crew, shrugs his shoulders with a contented smile across his face. I look to Joss for an explanation.

"Easy, my boy," Joss calls out, looking over her shoulder to me with a smirk. In a lower voice, she murmurs, "The real party is behind the vault."

We are at the end of a dimly lit hallway now, lined with red carpet and surrounded by dark wood-panel walls. In front of us is a big, golden vault door that the security twists the lever effortlessly until a heavy clank, indicating the door is unlocked, can be heard. As the door groans open, I chuckle, realizing the joke. Cool air prickles my skin, laced with perfume and top-shelf liquor. A bassline rumbles through my sternum as the new, moody, and luxe atmosphere is revealed. A beauty floats into our view.

She's in an attire that is much different from the ones in the main lobby. She's equally gorgeous as the others, her deep brown skin had a slight sheen to it under the small light at the door, and she wore a bright yet seductive smile that was surrounded by bold red-painted lips. What set her apart from the hostess before was the catsuit she wore. The bottom mimics black high-waist leggings while the top turns into sheer skintone material. The choice of material exposed the curvature of her full breasts, with black glistening jewels creating an intricate design over her nipples.

"Welcome to The Vault, the best secret in town. I'm Coco," she welcomes in a sultry tone."The way we keep things air-tight in here is by retrieving your phones." With a smirk, she proffers her hand. "Gentlemen…"

"What the fuck," I whisper with much amusement. The guys exchange curious looks before looking to Joss, who tilts her head to the woman in a way to do as instructed. My eyes slit curiously as a hint of something simmers in the way that Joss acknowledges Coco. We oblige, passing our phones to Coco, who in turn passes them to the security guard who brought us back here. He places them in a black velvet bag with a long number on it.

Joss is the last to give up her device. I watch as she flips it in the direction of the hostess, performing a mean stare down with her. I move my eyes to Coco, confirming she's giving Joss the same eye, and watch her lips slightly pucker at her. It seems like a silent game is going on between them that none of us is privy to. I chuckle, peeping all the signs confirming my suspicions as Joss stuffs a hand in her slacks pocket and runs the other over her curly top face. Wetting her lips, she asks, "See you around?"

I watch as the hostess flicks a sexy grin to Joss before softly saying, "Don't you always, Jocelyn?" and then turns on her heels and gestures for us to follow, her ass length ponytail swaying with her ample hips. And right there, it hits me—whatever they thought they were hiding, the history between them was loud and clear.

"Jocelyn, eh?" I ask, hinting at my curiosity about how Joss knew her well enough that she named her by her full legal name.

Joss shrugs, still wearing the satisfied smirk that settled on her face after Coco's confirmation. Her swagger holds her confidence as she offers, "Yeah, she's about the only woman I let call me Jocelyn, but she knows Big Joss very well."

My eyes grow big, and I raspberry before my laughter bursts, colliding with the low rumble of bass filling the room, thinking about how Joss is turning these women out. I don't doubt her; Joss exudes masculine energy that I've witnessed turn the eyes of the most heterosexual woman, but personally meeting one of her women and catching the energy between the two was something else.

Coco leads us through the lightly populated speakeasy. There's no jazz playing, but a sultry popular song that's heavy in bass, and unlike the stark, bright atmosphere of the main lobby, there's only a blue glow that takes over the room, making it moody yet discreet. Even with the dimness, I could see that it was a full house, but not packed like sardines. There were small plush sectionals, perfect for a party of 2 or 4, spaced out in the center of the room in front of a T-shaped stage. Coco stops in front of the destination, an elevated sectional suited for at least ten people, complete with an L-Shape leather sectional, a long table in the center displaying two bottles of bubbly and glasses. Two other hostesses were waiting for us, equally beautiful and in the same attire as Coco, who takes over after she leaves.

Once we are up the few steps and into our sectional, Joss swaggers over to Denzel and squeezes his shoulders, yelling over the sultry music, "You ready for the best show of your life?"

"Yeaahh, I guess so," he drags out with a somewhat nervous laugh. "I don't know what you guys got me into…"

Before he can finish his sentence, Deacon and Jace jump in, egging him to loosen up, Deacon giving him playful punches to his chest while Jace ruffles the waves on his head. Feeling the energy of getting Denzel out of his box, I grab one of the uncorked bottles and amble over to him.

"Okay, Chief, we are off the clock, and the ladies are an hour away..." The mention of Nina's Bridal Cruise going on right now ushers in a quick dip in my heart, acknowledging the lack of communication from Joni, but I whisk it away for the sake of keeping the momentum alive. "Loosen up because this is your last night of the free world! Chug it!"

I jab my arm out towards Denzel, placing the bottle in his face while the rest of the crew chants, "Chug it!" After ridding his reluctance, he gave, snatching the bottle from my hand and chugging down the bottle of bubbly, spillage dripping from the sides of his mouth. The crew breaks out in cheers. When he comes up for air, he wipes the trickle of liquid from his mouth with the back of his hand, completely void of his previous apprehension. His face is now lit with mischief, the kind that affirms he's in on the plan to make this a night to remember.

Yeah, this might be a certified crazy night that Denzel won't remember — but I'll keep the receipts.

"That's right! If he liked it, he should've put a ring on it! Show that rock off, girl!" I hyped Nina up as Beyoncé's iconic song blares through the boat's sound system.

Nina wiggles her hips to the beat, not caring about how much her bodycon dress is inching up her thighs. She's all smiles, her bejeweled "Bride" crown gleaming just as much as her engagement rings. She's waving into the camera of Fallon's phone, mimicking the wave Beyoncé performs in the video for this song. I dip under Fallon's arm, but not too far to construe the footage and pull at the hem of Nina's dress, just before it raises high enough to give a glimpse of her woo-haa. I snicker as I secure her, thinking Denzel wouldn't be too happy for his future wife to go viral for an accidental peekaboo. Maybe I shouldn't have done that because Nina loses her balance, falling back into the lap of her other bridesmaids.

Typical Nina mishap, but what a perfect ending to the video.

The slight rocking of the boat as Nina collapses into a giggling fit reminds me that we are in the middle of Lovey's Bay. Nina continued with her idea to have her bachelorette on a nighttime cruise of the bay, despite my warnings of potential killer seagulls. Luck was in our favor, because there hadn't been a seagull in sight for the hour we've been on the water. The only thing that's been permeating the warm, salty air is the sounds of Nina's playlist of Beyoncé songs that commemorate the reason for the party: the big, bountiful love between Nina and Denzel that will become officially legal in two weeks.

Seamlessly, the previous song transitions to a song of Beyoncé singing about her love being on top. Nina struggles but pushes up from her sunken position in between her bridesmaids, crooning, "Oh, this is my soooooong!"

She proceeds to sway her hips and her hands above her head as she sings. I chuckle at my girl's pure joy and find a seat beside Fallon as we watch her bask in it.

Fallon leans in and whispers, "Girl, how do you think she's gonna act when we turn this sappy shit off for some slow grind music for our dancers?"

"I don't know, but one of us needs to make sure she is seated and now by the edge of the boat. All our men are in Regency and nowhere close enough to her rescue," I snort, playing the possible scene of Nina accidentally falling overboard at the shock of the half-naked men coming up from the bottom level in my head. Skating in behind that thought is an image of Tevin's face, and my stomach lurches with a longing for him.

Almost like she had front row seats to my thoughts, Fallon asks, "Speaking of our men…have you cleared things up with your man?" I jerk my head to her in surprise. She giggles and answers my silent question. "The way your eyes clouded over, I knew you were thinking about Tevin. And from the look on your face, no, you did not clear it up."

I open my mouth to argue my reasoning for not having the conversation necessary with Tevin, but no words come out. I have none. Embarrassment still settles in my bones for how I acted, and shock still pits in my stomach from Tevin's response to Malik. The highly active emotions all stay present in me because of the memory of Nova witnessing it all.

"Girl, this could've been resolved by now," Fallon says in disbelief at my silent admittance. "So you both showed your ass a little bit. Okay, and?"

That's when I found my words. "And we did it in front of Nova. This is the type of scenario I didn't want her witnessing. She'd already witnessed enough chaos between me and her Dad. I want her to see differently. To see peace."

Fallon purses her lip as she deadpans. "So, how is she gonna see that if you aren't talking to Tevin?"

"What are you two over here whispering about?" Nina comes and stoops in front of us, resting an elbow on either of our knees. Her glossy eyes show just how inebriated she is as she swings her head from Fallon to me and then back to Fallon. "Don't get all quiet now. It's my day, so answer *me*."

Her smile is just as wobbly as her legs, and she tries to balance herself and point both pointer fingers to her chest. Seeing the fail happening before us, Fallon and I grab an elbow and pull Nina up, making a small space between us for her to sit. Her head falls back briefly as she lets out a "whew" before she levels and looks between us. "Okay, now spill."

Fallon and I look at each other and giggle at Nina's silliness before Fallon offers up the tea. "Oh, I was just chewing Joni out because she still has not had a conversation with Tevin since…"

"Ms. Trinidad?" Nina blurts out and then giggles as she covers her mouth. My jaw drops, playfully offended by her reference to the character from a classic Martin episode. Apologetically, Nina mutters, "I'm sorry."

I roll my eyes, muttering, "Whatever," the words crawling out with a sigh.

"I need you two to get it together. The wedding is in two weeks…the dinner is in one," Nina reminds, putting a finger up for each week. "I need everything picture perfect for my big day."

"Okay, Bridezilla," I quip, jokingly. She slants her eyes at me, silently telling me she means it.

Fallon sits up to look at me. "I don't get it. What's your hang-up? It's Tevin."

"It's not Tevin." Nina leans into Fallon's space, cutting off her view of me. Fallon playfully nudges her back, giving her the stank face. It's clear Nina doesn't catch on to her mishap, because she keeps talking. "It's not about Tevin. It's about Malik, isn't it?"

Nina tilts her head, daring me to tell her that she's wrong. I move my eyes down to my fidgeting fingers, before I meet her stare with narrowed eyes as I scoff out my lie, "It is, but not like how you're making it."

"Oh, it's everything like I'm making it," Nina confirms, pointing a finger at me. "You are projecting your experience with Malik onto Tevin. Malik was a cheater, cheater, pumpkin eater, and now, because a situation that mirrors one you've been through with Malik happens, you automatically put Tevin in the same box as Malik. Except, he's nothing like him….at all."

Nina nods her head affirmingly. It stuns me so much how she read me for filth that I pause to dissect her analogy.

She's right. Tevin has never given me a reason to doubt him. He's been down for me before we even put labels on us, and he's proven it—in front of both Avery and Malik. Why would he do all of that if he was going to turn around and play in my face?

"I am going to put on the hat you normally wear…" Nina says, donning an invisible hat on her head. She dips her head to me, "…The 'tell it like it is' hat." Fallon lets out a quiet "oop" before she peels herself up from the chair and mouths she'll be right back, mischief glimmering in her eyes.

I'm zapped back into Nina's rant as she sits up tall and clears her throat, "You once said, 'I know when I have a good thing when I have it, even if it's just good dick…" Nina's mimic of my voice causes me to scoff and chuckle at the same time. She looks at me with a smize and a lifted arch brow. "Did you forget your own words? Don't lose your good thing over a Miss Trinidad. Gina would nevaaa….and I know my Joni ain't."

Nina wags her finger exaggeratedly, curving it into an oblong 'S' through the air, and we all fall into a laughing fit. I don't know if it's Nina's drunken state that makes this whole scene funny or if she actually remembered what I once told her verbatim. I wasn't sure, but I am certain that she told no lies. Gina did not let a thirsty Miss Trinidad seduce her man away; she put on her boxing gloves and fought for her man. Now, I think I've done enough jabbing with my words alone to Shelby on the day of the orientation. The only fighting I need to do now is to fight past my ego and be vulnerable with Tevin. Express my truths and my apologies.

The abrupt change in mood from bubbly Beyonce to a sultry Tank song makes me pull my attention from Nina to Fallon standing at the foot of the steps that lead to the lower level. Holding on to the rails on either side of her, she shimmies her shoulders as she scans and smirks across the deck of women, landing her final look on Nina.

"Beyonce's fun, but a little Tank for some men with loaded tanks is far more entertaining," Fallon teases as she completes her climb back onto the deck. Following behind her are three muscular Gods dressed in chaps and undergarments that hid no surprises. Extending her hand like she's Keke Shepard, she sings, "Oh, fellasssss…!"

Realizing this is the moment I needed to secure Nina from a possible incident, I extend my hand over her midsection. She, in turn, wacks my hand away, standing quickly to her feet.

"Oh my God…you got me three Bolos?!?" Nina squeals. She collapses her hands to her chest like she has been surprised with the sweetest gift of her life. We all look at each other, clearly understanding her reference to the infamous Real Housewives of Atlanta male dancer, and fall out laughing, including the men as they amble towards her.

Not the sweetest gift, but hands down the nastiest one we'll ever give her.

2:43 am early Sunday Morning

Joni: Hey. You up?

Tevin: Hey Babe. Yeah. You good?

Tevin: I miss you.

Joni: I miss you too.

Joni: I'm sorry too. Can we talk…in person?

Tevin: I'm sorry too. Of course, babe. Tonight?

Joni: I wish. We are nursing Nina out of her drunken state. Lol

Joni: Wednesday? I have a lot to do at the top of the week. You know, Nova and wedding stuff for Nina.

Tevin: Oh wow, okay, lol. Wednesday it is.

Tevin: I love you.

Joni: I love you too.

28

TEVIN

I've checked my calendar several times today to make sure that today wasn't the 13th and on a Friday, because what the fuck? It's only Wednesday, and all hell has broken loose in Lovey's Bay. There have been one emergency call after another, and I'm relieved when twenty minutes have passed and no sign of an emergency. My stomach is now reaching my back and is demanding to be fueled. I stroll into the firehouse kitchen and pull open the white refrigerator door, grabbing the light 12-pack of eggs, some cheese, and snatch the loaf of bread from the top of the fridge. My mouth waters at the thought of a simple egg and cheese sandwich.

My suspicion of the light egg carton is confirmed when I open it, revealing only two eggs. I wanted four.

Beggars can't be choosy, but they can sure as hell complain.

"Aye! Who ate all the eggs and didn't replace the carton?!" My voice echoes through the open space, and I hear low mumbles in response. I turn around, bugging my eyes at the crew scattered from the dining table to the living room quarter.

Deacon strolls in with a half smile as if he had something slick to say. I turn back to the countertop, grabbing an egg with either hand. He slaps my back as he peers down at the nearly empty carton before me. "Technically, it's not empty, but once you eat those two, it will be, making you the one who needs to replenish."

"You're an asshole," I mumble, nudging him out of the way so that I could crack the eggs into the bowl I had out. From my periphery, I can see him getting comfortable leaning with his back against the counter.

He shrugs, playing into my insult. "I try to be."

"Man, what the hell is going on today? It's like everyone chose today to fuck up something."

Deacon blows out a breath. "I don't know, but this only tells me that the rest of the day is going to follow suit."

I move over to turn the electrical eye on where my pan of butter is resting, mumbling, "Man, I hope not. I need to get off on time today."

My 24-hour shift today ends at 5 pm, and I've been

anxious about it. I hadn't seen Joni for far too long, and I am ready for us to get past the road bump we encountered at the elementary school. I hated that Joni shut me out afterwards because it didn't allow me the opportunity to clear up what was supposed to be a fun surprise, and also make it absolutely certain that nothing was going on with Shelby and me. I even made sure to close that door later that evening with a cordial "It was nice knowing you, but goodbye" text to Shelby. However, the way Joni shut down, I knew there had to be more to it than being mad at the fucked up scene she walked up on. Denzel confirmed that during the bachelor party.

"Man, that dude Malik did a number on her from what Nina told me," I remembered him slurring after finally slumping down on the couch of our section.

He'd been doing as a bachelor should do, enjoying being the center of attention to multiple busty dancers showing him love. He was respectful about it, though, never touching them, and when they got too close to his crotch, politely waving them off. A fucking gentleman.

When he chimed in, it was after he caught wind of Deacon and me conversing about why I was sitting in the corner, not being the party animal I'm known to be. I partook in the festivities, but after a while, my mind drifted into the abyss of thoughts that included Joni, and I felt fucked up about being out here without there being peace within my relationship. I remembered zoning in on

Denzel, waiting for him to fill me in with more of what he knew. I thank the liquor Gods later because he did continue.

"I don't know, Nina and Joni seemed to have gotten to the bottom of the barrel before us, because Joni's ex was just as bad as Nina's. Instead of leaving her high and dry like Nina's ex, he kept her around while he cheated on her—several times."

I knew this piece of information. Joni and I have talked about that, but it still didn't clue me in on why she went radio silent on me. I remember those very thoughts, and then Deacon chimed in with insight that stuck with me.

"It's a trauma response," he said, very controlled as he looked at me. "Fallon had a similar response to me. She fought against her feelings for me because of the shit she went through with her ex and some of her parental issues, too. No matter where the trauma comes from, it manifests into thinking everyone is like that until they realize they are in safe places now."

I joked about Deacon's new nickname being Dr. Feel Good, but I was listening and taking notes. He shared how he just continued to be a safe space for Fallon and listened to her as she peeled back her layers, and I wanted to do that for Joni. I don't know what kind of voodoo she worked on me, but I was a man who wanted to do whatever it took to make sure she was mine and that she felt like I was her safe space. So when she texted me that night, I couldn't help but blurt out that I missed and loved her, and quickly agreed that we would talk today.

However, after I scoffed down my sandwich, the idea of me getting off on time started to look improbable when the digital siren alert went off.

"First Responders Needed at Sunny Bay Elementary School…"

That's all that I heard before I took off to the engine, meeting Deacon, Joss, and another crew member, Farris. In minutes, the engine roars and the blare of the siren fills the streets of Lovey's Bay as we make our way to the school.

"What's the emergency?" I ask after we are about five minutes into the ten-minute drive to the school.

"Some kids were playing in a tree near the playground, and one of them fell. Sounds like a broken leg," Deacon responds with an even tone. After seeing everything possible, nothing seems to faze him when it comes to emergencies.

My brows pucker as I sigh, "Damn. What the hell are they doing in a tree, though?"

"C'mon, Tev, like you didn't play in trees when you were a kid," I hear Joss say from behind.

I turn to her. "Yeah, I did, but I never climbed one unless I knew I could bring my ass back down."

"No judgment. We don't know what happened," Deacon reminds, making the last turn that takes us down the road to the school. "Anything could have happened. Let's just hope for the best."

When we pull into the parking lot, I take note of the crowd of people at a shady tree just outside the playground. It's only then that the thought of Nova comes to mind, and for some reason, my chest caves, and I can feel my pulse quickening. *Could it be her?* The question plagues my mind as my body springs from the truck, full of antsy energy as soon as the engine turns off. I pray she isn't the one hurt as I forge forward, leading the team, but as the crowd parts at our arrival, a hard thud hits the center of my chest. It's Nova.

"Shit," I hiss, quickening my steps. The closer I get, the louder her pain-filled screams and cries drive my feet into a light jog until I reach her side.

"It hurts! It hurts!"

"It's okay, it's okay, help is here."

I recognize the voice, and when she turns her head, I see that it's Shelby cradling Nova. She looks at me with shock just as my move to kneel by Nova's side stutters. It's the first time I've seen her since my text, and the subtle disappointment glimmers in her eyes before her worry for Nova clouds her face. Tightening my lips and proceeding to kneel, I nod my head in a way to ask her to make room. She does, giving me space and a moment with Nova.

"Supernova..." My voice takes on a sappy tone, evidence of the pull Nova has over my heart in a matter of months. I wouldn't change the feeling for anything, especially experiencing the shift in pained expression as she looks to me like I was her hero.

"Mr. Tevin...is-is my mommy here?" she whimpers, reaching her hands up and pulling me to her into a hug.

My chest aches as her whimpers fill my ears and her tears wet the side of my face. "I don't know, baby girl, but I'm here and we are going to make sure you are okay before the ambulance gets here."

She gasps, and a muffled sob leaves her. "I have to go in an ambulance?"

I pull away slightly, looking at her mangled leg and wince, the pain she's experiencing causing my stomach to cringe. I look back at her, mustering a smile. "Yes, you'll go to the hospital in an ambulance, but you will be fine. I promise."

She sobs harder before she blinks a flood of tears down her face as she asks, "Will you come with me?"

My heart broke a little harder knowing I may not be able to go with her. Just as I formulate a way to tell her I can't, I hear a masculine voice before I see the owner of it.

"Daddy's here, babygirl!"

Malik rushes to the opposite side of Nova, squatting down and taking my place as I respectfully pull back. Nova's grasp clings to me a moment longer before she realizes her Dad is right there. That's when he cradled her and slowly stood up, returning to my professionalism. Just as I do, paramedics hustle in to stabilize Nova's leg and prep her for the ride to the hospital.

I'm relieved that I didn't have to tell her I wouldn't be able to go with her, but my chest still ached because I couldn't. More than anything, I want to hop into that ambulance and make sure she's good, but her father is here. As much as I wasn't feeling him as a person, I can tell he loves Nova just as much as I'm starting to love her. It's his time to be her hero, but I would make sure to check on my Supernova at the end of my shift.

I was in The Coves with Nina and her wedding planner when I missed Malik's call about Nova's accident. Being her maid of honor, I have been her right hand when Denzel couldn't be a part of it, and the visit to the Country Club for the final walk-through of the bridal party dinner space was one of those things.

Nina chose not to do the bridal party dinner the night before the wedding, as traditionally done, and will be hosting it this Friday. She's been so nervous about something happening, whether it be her having a clutzy moment or just something scheduled off that would not allow her big day to go smoothly. I wish she weren't so much in a frenzy about something going wrong, but could I blame her? No, not after her track record. So, we went and finalized the menu early to ease one of her worries.

While Nina spoke with her wedding planner in the hallway just before we were to leave, I peered over to the empty ballroom where Nina would hold her reception. I tiptoe into the room, scanning it as I imagine all the round tables, clothed in white linen, filling the space, with the gaudy but gorgeous crystal chandelier sparkling in the center as the first dance takes place. When I move my eyes from the chandelier to where the spotlight would shine on the newlyweds, a ghost of an image of me being the bride and Tevin being the groom fades in.

The idea of me eventually getting married has been a lost cause for some time. After dealing with Malik, I was almost content with the possibility of it not happening. I'd become so comfortable with the peace that comes with not having to struggle to make love work in order to be married. That's until these feelings for Tevin began to creep in. There weren't supposed to be any feelings, just fucking, but who doesn't let the guard of their heart slip by accident and fall for their lover? I don't know anyone who would say they didn't. Hell, I've seen it happen with Fallon—and now it's happening to me.

Tevin makes me wonder what it would be like if we just let this love thing do what it wants between us. Shoot, maybe one day we will get married, if he doesn't get rid of me. He wants someone younger. Somehow, by the way he can't get enough of me, I highly doubt that will happen, that's if I don't get my shit together and have this much-needed conversation with him today.

Remembering that I am supposed to meet Tevin this evening, I pull my phone from my purse to check the time. It's almost five thirty, and I remind myself that he would be getting off in about thirty minutes when I see the trail of texts from Malik. The most current text asked if I am almost at the hospital. Seeing 'hospital' makes me scroll down to the first text, which tells me that Nova has been hurt.

Three hours ago.

Before it can all register, my heels are clacking against the marble as I rush back into the hallway. Sensing my urgency, Nina looks up with confusion in her wide eyes.

"Nova's been hurt," I breathe and rush past Nina, but not before she grabs hold of my arm.

"Oh, my God, what happened?"

"I don't know!" I yelled, ripping my arm from her grasp.

When I realized how hostile my words came out to

Nina's genuine concern, I let out a sharp breath in an attempt to regain some composure.

"Honestly, that doesn't matter to me right now. I just have to get to my baby."

Nina shakes her head frantically as she touches my hand, not saying anything more except for me to be safe and to call her when I can.

The drive to the hospital was agonizing. It didn't help my nerves that I was rushing to the hospital during the tail end of rush hour. Eventually, I had to remind myself that I needed to breathe. Her father is there with her. One thing I can't take away from Malik is that he's a good father, and I can count on him to make sure Nova is well when I'm not present. So, while I inch through the traffic, I call Malik and explain to him my delay.

"It's all good," Malik assures. "She's doing better… resting. But when I got her, she was a wreck."

I breathe, "I bet. I'm so disappointed I wasn't there—"

He interrupts me with my reassurance, "But I was. She had one of us there for her. That's all that matters."

There's a silence that settles through the speakers of the car, leaving me with only the quiet purr of my engine. Malik breaks the silence with a crack to voice as he says, "That guy, Tevin, was there…" I can hear him push out a breath while I hold mine and let my heart swell at the thought of Tevin being on my daughter's side. Malik whines out, "Why's he always around like that…?"

His question sounds loaded, but I only respond to the obvious.

"Tevin's a firefighter. A first responder. Why wouldn't he possibly be there?" I jerk my head back and screw up my face as if he can see me. I even glance down at the touchscreen display, like I will see Malik's audacity on his face. Malik says nothing, the cat clearly catching his tongue. I take the exit to the hospital before I speak again. "And Tevin isn't finding his way around. He is around and will be around for a long time. You're going to have to get used to it. As a matter of fact, there's not much for you to get used to. We co-parent well, and that's all that we do."

I'm pulling up to the hospital when I finish my speech and dismiss Malik from my line so that the valet can park my car. Finding the nearest elevator, I ride it up to the Children's Floor. When the elevator dings and the door slides open, this is when my nerves get the best of me. There were nurses everywhere, and hospital room numbers were displayed on lit signage along the long stretch of the hallway. One face slowed the beat of my heart but ushered in the tears.

"Tevin…" I breathe as I run into his outstretched arms. I exhale a calming breath as my tears wet his fire department t-shirt.

He rubs his hands up and down my back, and I feel him press his lips to the top of my head. I hook my arms under his, squeezing him tightly, never wanting to not feel my head on his chest for this long ever again, while also needing to hear his calm heartbeat in my ear. It was confirmation that Nova really is okay.

I look up at him, blinking away my tears, whispering, "I heard you were there."

He wipes away my eye with his thumb as he looks me in the eyes. I can see his eyes wince slightly, like he is thinking about the moment. His voice rasps, "Yeah. When I got to her, it was clear she had a broken leg. She was in a lot of pain."

I take in a shaky breath at the details and feel my heart break thinking about my child in pain. Tevin leans down and pecks my lips with a soothing kiss.

"Supernova's strong," he whispers. "She did just fine…and Malik was there to help her through it."

I scan his eyes for answers. Answers to how it played out with him and Malik. His eyes stayed neutral, giving away nothing. Tevin knows me well and can tell what I am doing, so he speaks.

"I got here about thirty minutes ago. Deacon let me leave early so I could check on you guys. I didn't know you hadn't made it here yet, so I was surprised to run into just him when I got here…" My eyes widen, anticipating some shit. Tevin tilts his head and continues, "…

Nothing popped off, but we did talk, you know, man-to-man. I let him know I wasn't going anywhere and not trying to replace him in Nova's life…just adding the two of you's life."

I could let Tevin have me right here…right now…if we weren't here for the sake of my baby girl. Hearing him yet again stake his claim in my life—in our life—makes my heart shudder. I push up on the balls of my feet and kiss him, sweetly, before giving his bottom lip a little suck. I have to push away to keep from crossing the PG line.

In my periphery, I see Malik ambling down the hallway towards us. When we make eye contact, he lowers his eyes and runs his hand over his waves. Tevin takes notice of my gaze and lets go of my waist with one hand so that we are both facing Malik as he nears.

"I'm gonna head out," he cracks. If I'm not mistaken, disappointment lingers in his tone. He looks to Tevin and then to me. "I waited until she fell asleep."

I nod my head, giving him a faint yet gracious smile. "Thanks, Malik. We're good from here. I'll let you know how she does overnight."

He doesn't say anything else, just nods and gives Tevin one more sullen look before he strolls past us.

29

—

JONI

Clink! Clink! Clink!

"May I have your attention, please. First, I want to say…"

Nina stands before us, giving her after-dinner speech. She's at the head of the rectangular linened table set for twelve, the soon-to-be newlyweds and each bridesmaid and groomsmen. We're seated in traditional seating, Nina and Denzel at either end of the table, and the bridesmaids on one side of the table with the groomsmen on the opposite end. Needing order, Nina sat us across from those we'd walk the aisle with on the wedding day. Deacon would've sat across from me, him being the Best Man and me the Maid of Honor, but I twisted Nina's arm for Tevin to sit across from me, at least for the wedding party dinner. Begrudgingly, she obliged and hissed that she would not be changing the aisle structure for this. Of course, I wouldn't ask her to do that, but today, I had to be able to peer across the table at my man.

Since Nova's accident, I haven't had much quality time with Tevin. Nova's injury allowed her to go home the following morning, but she still needed my undivided attention. I took off the rest of the week to tend to her, fully prepared to do it on my own. I was surprised by Tevin when I reached the lobby of the hospital. I remember pushing Nova and nearly running her into him if it wasn't for her squealing his name. It was a pleasant surprise, but my chest had had enough surprises for me, and it began palpitations, thinking he had met me there to tell me something awful had happened. That wasn't the case. He came to help. He insisted on escorting us from the hospital.

I thought we were going to my apartment, but when we pulled up to his townhome, I whipped my head to him and frowned.

"I thought you two could come here while Nova heals," I remember him stating. He'd placed his hand over mine and enclosed it in a way that felt like he was soothing my questions away. My questions remained.

"Tevin. You have a whole roommate. How—"

"Jace moved out a couple of weeks ago," he calmly

slid in, silencing my rant. "The room is clean and on the first floor. Nova can stay there, so she doesn't have to worry about steps. That's the main reason I suggest you two stay here instead of your apartment. You don't live on the first level."

"I have an elevator," I quip. "We can take the elevator up and that's all we'd have to worry about—"

"What if there's a fire emergency?" he shot back at me, pinning me with serious eyes. "Then I'd be worried."

"We don't…" My words failed me when he leaned over to me, placing his right hand on the back of my seat. I don't know if he's attempting to shield Nova from hearing what he said next.

"Joni. I know you are used to being in charge, but let me take the lead on this one. Let me make sure my Lil' Bit and our Supernova are good."

God, this man. If you had told me that taking Tevin seriously would've brought out this side of Tevin, I wouldn't have believed you, not even six months ago. Tevin has always been full of jokes and fun, which is what I loved the most about him—until I met this side of him. Now, he takes charge in the best way. Not forceful but in dutiful action. He makes me feel secure in a way that I feel like I can soften and know he has both me and Nova's best interests at heart. So, I closed my mouth and let him temporarily move us in.

At first, I felt out of my element. Tevin worked a 24-hour shift in the first two days of our stay. His being away from the house allowed me to get acclimated, comfortable…and miss him. It took Nova no time because Frenchie, now her animal BFF, stayed by her side. By the end of day two, having him with us for the full day, I'd learned to enjoy having a partner, even if temporary. An inkling within me hoped it wouldn't be temporary.

Needless to say, the wedding dinner is the first alone time Tevin and I have had since Nova and I moved in. Nova is with her father for the weekend, which means we have no one to tend to but each other. The way Tevin kept giving me seductive, hooded eyes across the table during Nina's speech, I knew he had the same ideas floating in his mind as I did.

I'm going to have my way with this man tonight…

"So tonight, we want to thank you all for being our friends, our confidants, and putting up with us through this crazy ride. Thank you!"

The soft round of applause that consumes the table after Nina's speech settles me back into reality. I look to Nina, who is now holding her champagne flute above her head, positioned to toast. We all follow suit, grabbing our glasses and giving collaborative salutations before soft R&B music began to flow through the speakers of the Country Club's private dining room.

I'd finished my glass when I caught Tevin's eyes and the nod of his head directing me to come with him. He scoots from his chair and begins to walk towards the double doors that lead to the hallway. Quickly, I get up and follow suit. Within the quiet hum of the hallway, Tevin catches my hand and leads me to another room.

The ballroom is pin-drop quiet, besides the muffle of the music from the room we'd just exited, and about five degrees cooler, instantly causing my skin to prickle with goosebumps. It's mostly dark in the room, except for maybe two or three overhead lights above. It's enough light to illuminate the linened tables, bare of chairs. I assume that it's either being prepared for an event or being broken down after one.

We walk further into the room and approach the first table to our left. Tevin lifts me and places me on top of the table before locking me in with his hands straddling the table on either side of me. The kiss he plants on my lips is so soft, but it ignites a warmth in my center. I don't know how much longer we will make it here before it's time for us to depart.

Tevin pulls away, gazing dreamily into my eyes. "I just wanted some alone time with you."

"The feeling's mutual," I snicker, running my hand down the side of his tie. "We haven't had much of that lately…with everything."

"Everything" wasn't just Nova. Before then, I was in

my shell, shunning him and not talking about my feelings. Tevin nods his head in a way that says he understands.

"Yeah. We still haven't had our talk."

"We haven't," I agree, looking down to my lap and playing with the pearl satin of my dress before looking back at his expectant eyes. "About the orientation thing…I was out of line. I didn't even ask you what the situation was about."

Tevin exhales, "It's not all your fault. I could've told you something, but that would've taken away from my surprise. I wanted to surprise you and Nova by being there, but I guess that blew up in my face."

I blink my eyes wide, totally unprepared for the news that he planned to be there and surprise us. This news makes my stomach hollow in guilt for my actions, and then I think about the read Nina gave me the night of the bachelorette cruise.

"Tevin, you're different," I say in a near whisper. My eyes are on my fiddling fingers as I ready myself to be vulnerable. I move my eyes to his again. "I'm not used to someone being solely into me and wanting everything that comes with me." I pause and then chuckle, "I'm used to cheaters like Malik."

I can see Tevin's jaw clench as he slowly nods. "Well, I'm not him. All I want is you…and Shelby knows that now, too. I made sure to nip that in the bud that night."

Tevin's certainty stirs an insecurity within me for some reason, making butterflies flutter in my chest, and I ask, "Tevin, how do you know you'll always feel like that? I'm five years older than you."

There it goes. Not only is there a simmering feeling of maybe not being enough to keep his eyes from wandering away from me, but that maybe the thrill will go away when our age difference settles in after the fun of us has died down. The way Tevin's eyes slant with incredulity and then kiss his teeth relieves the slight tension in my center.

"I don't see any of that. You know why…?" He leans in and nuzzles my neck to the side, planting a sensual kiss there before whispering into my ear, "What I feel for you isn't temporary. It's something I want to feel for a lifetime."

My eyes drift close to the sound of his sweet, earnest words, and suddenly, the dimly lit dining room we crept into transforms into another galaxy within my imagination as I bask in the warming sensation that showers my skin as he trails kisses up my jawline. And when his full lips finally meet mine, they don't immediately touch. Our soft, champagne-infused breaths linger, creating a magnetic force between us, our energies tugging and pulling. I can hear the faint sound of Nina on the mic in the other room when our lips finally fuse, reminding me that our private moment collides with a wedding dinner we are supposed to be partaking in. That memory becomes a distant one as I get lost in the moment. With Tevin's arms cradling me to him, I part my lips, inviting our tongues to play within an intimate playground.

"Clap it up! It's our guy's big day!"

Deacon rallies the room of groomsmen up into clapping as Denzel walks in from the bedroom of the suite at The Pelican Hotel. He swaggers out of the room, holding open the jacket to his dress uniform to show off the crisp white dress shirt, starched pants, and spit-shined shoes. Chief is beaming bright enough to light up the room, which is full of natural light provided by the high noon sun.

The claps turn into testosterone-filled hoots when Denzel stops in the middle of the circle and spins, giving a 360-degree view of his spiffiness before we huddle around him, playfully shoving him. You'd think we just won the Super Bowl with the celebrating we are doing, as opposed to getting ready for Denzel's wedding.

"Don't mess up my suit before I see my lady, now," Denzel laughs, finding his way out of the circle.

"Man, ain't nobody gonna be able to wrinkle that super starched suit!" I joke. The room falls into laughter as I approach him and squeeze his shoulder. "All jokes aside, you're sharp, Chief. The groom's glow looks good on you!"

"Thank you, brother," Denzel says. He scans over us all. "You all look good. Thank you for cleaning up so well, brothers."

In a few steps, Denzel makes his way back to the semicircle of his groomsmen. We are dressed sharp, if I must admit. Denzel and I are dressed in our dress uniforms along with the Chief, decorated with our medallions and gold badges. It was his request by way of Nina, and I had no quarrels with it; it saved me some money. The other three groomsmen were dressed in sleek black tuxedos and white shirts that easily blended with our attire.

After a few moments of camaraderie, the group splits, leaving Deacon, me, and Denzel in the middle of the floor. He pulls out an oblong, hard leather case from his pocket, flicking its latch to reveal three hefty cigars. He looks between the two of us, proffering, "I was going to wait until after the ceremony, but why the hell not? Fellas?"

In separate forms, Denzel and I agree and follow

Deacon out onto the suite's patio. Immediately, the crashing waves take over the chatter of the guys in the room as I close the sliding door, followed by the click of the torch lighter lighting the end of our respective cigars. I'm not much of a cigar smoker, but I puff, taking in the liquored smoke.

"So, do you have any advice, OG?" Denzel asks Deacon with a joking air in his question.

Deacon is looking out over the bay when Denzel asks and blows out the puff of smoke that filled his cheeks before he turns around. A short chuckle escapes him before he says, "Shiit, I haven't been married more than a year yet. Your advice is as good as mine. Shit, we might be better off asking Little Tev No-Campbell."

They both shoot inquiring eyes at me, and I rear my head back, totally caught off guard. I nearly choke on my cigar's air, making the guys crack up. I recover after a few clearing coughs.

"What y'all looking at me for? I just got Joni to let me be Big Daddy." I put my hands in the air and swivel my hips like I am working Joni's middle. The guys laugh again.

"About damn time," Deacon says, mid-laugh. "I was beginning to worry about your lockdown game."

I tilt my head, side-eyeing him, and twist my mouth at the blasphemy. He shrugs and takes another puff of his cigar before growing slightly more serious. "All jokes aside, I don't even know if there's any advice that can be given. Every relationship is different." He pauses as he looks up in thought before he looks to us again. "If I had to give any advice, I'd just say to listen. Women will tell you what they need, whether directly or indirectly. Listen to their words and their body language. And…keep in the forefront, it's not just you anymore. Your lady is a part of you and your decisions. Treat her like your equal, but still lead your family. You know what I mean?"

"Yeah, I get it."

While Denzel daps Deacon up and receives more congratulations from him, I stand there pondering Deacon's words. Even though the sage advice was for Denzel, it hit home for me. While I joked about Joni just starting to get comfortable in our relationship fully, I took Deacon's words to heart on how I should operate going forward. I see long-term with Joni, but I'm not ready to spring that on her just yet. I want to feel that I'm preparing for the long term before she sees it. I want her to know I'm taking her into account in a way she hadn't been used to before me. I want her to know I hear her just as much as I see her.

"You good, champ?"

Denzel's inquiry pulls me out of my thoughts, and I blink my eyes, finding him standing in front of me with a hand on my shoulder. His brows are slightly furrowed, furthering his question.

"Yeah, man," I breathe. "I just got caught up in my thoughts."

Denzel nods. "Cool. I thought you were taking Deacon's shit seriously."

"Man, nah! I know Deac don't do nothing but blow a bunch of smoke."

"Good, good," Denzel responds, shaking his head in approval. "Because we really do see the man you're growing into. You're not that goofy kid anymore. You taking on the volunteer squad and whipping them into professional shape is a big deal."

Hearing the big-up from my Chief pushes a proud smile across my face. The jokes, the fun, and the games are all good with my crew, but being respected by them and seen as someone who can lead, especially by Denzel, means a lot to me. I bob my head up and down as I let a breath of contentment out through my nose before I thank him, "Thanks, Chief. It means a lot."

He gives my shoulder another firm squeeze. "For sure. You deserve it…as well as what's next for you."

"What do you mean?" I question all while my face screws up.

Denzel releases his grip from my shoulder and stands square in front of me. His eyes settle slightly as if he's about to say something serious, while I can see a slight smile beckoning. He nods his head to me before he explains, "The city is opening a new station…in The

Coves. They ask me if I have anyone on my team ready for a leadership role. I put your name in the hat."

You would've thought I got gutted in the stomach the way the breath left my body. Just a few months ago, I was griping about them not taking me seriously, and here's Chief seriously offering my name for a leadership position. My adrenaline coursing through my veins sends an excited chill through my body, and I laugh under my breath, "Wow, for real, Chief?"

He chuckles at my surprise and reiterates, "For real. You're in school and you'll be well into finishing by the time they're ready to take flight. It'll be roughly six to nine months before that happens…and I'm not quite sure the leadership yet, but—"

"Shiid, no explanation needed! I'm down! Thanks, Chief!"

All the possibilities of this new opportunity rush through as I rush Denzel and bear hug him. The Cove is a whole new territory, albeit the land of luxury and affluence, but a place where I can start fresh in a big fucking way. Going from leading the volunteer squad to a leadership position with a brand new firehouse? That's Big Dawg shit. *That's Big Tev-typa shit.* No matter what the role may be, it means a lot for Chief to think of me as qualified and able.

The hug surprises Denzel, too, because he stumbles back before he hugs me back, chuckling, "No problem,

Brodie." He pats me on the back before he steps away so that he can look me in the eye. "You deserve, Tevin. Don't you forget that."

His words hit like steel in my chest, becoming a permanent fixture of approval that I not only needed but also earned. As we walk back into the suite, my mind is still flipping through the possibilities, with one taking precedence: how this could really level up the life I want to give Joni and Nova. A visual of Joni and Nova walking the almost white sands of that side of Lovey's Bay with smiles that make my chest expand flashes through my head.

I wonder what a small family home would cost out there? Who knows, maybe Joni and I can get our George and Wheezie and find us a nice deluxe house in The Coves.

"Aight, it's showtime, fellas! Our chariot awaits!"

Deacon's announcement brings me back to the moment, and I chuckle, catching myself getting swept away in my daydream, but I don't shy away from it. Instead, I poke my chest out a little more and take on a slight George Jefferson walk as I hum the catchy tune of "The Jefferson" as I follow the crew out of the suite.

JONI

From the moment the pianist pinged the first chord, I felt my heartstrings tugging on the vessels that led to my tear ducts, tempting the waterworks to start. You'd think I was getting married today as I took sips of my breath while I walked the candlelit, handmade aisle of the large patio of the Country Club.

"You okay?" I hear Deacon whisper when we are about halfway down the aisle. I glance up at him, realizing he's aware of my struggle to stay composed, and I nod quickly. I exhale quietly and let my eyes drift down to the ground, zeroing in on the candles.

Thank God these candles are fake, I think to myself, and then chuckle, glad for the comic relief to sweep away the emotions that threaten to take over me. The last thing we need is for Denzel to have to rescue Nina at their wedding.

When I take my position, Tevin and Fallon are nearing the point where they'd split and take their positions. Tevin and I meet eyes, and I catch the quick wink he sends. It turns the butterflies in my heart loose, and I drop my eyes, working to regain my composure. God, what has this man done? I'm not obsessed with my age, but when he looks at me, he makes me feel ten times younger. When he touches me, he makes my body feel like it's being touched in that manner for the first time. When I move my eyes back up and they snap back to his, there's that look again, but this time, it makes me feel optimistic.

You know, for a minute, I believed this kind of love may not find me. It's the type of love that makes you believe in the things you once gave up on, like, for me, having a husband of my own. I almost began to believe I'd be the "old lady in the shoe" like Whitney used to joke, lonely and by herself. But as I gaze into Tevin's eyes, I realize I was never alone, and those eyes always spoke to the optimistic side of me, even when I didn't believe.

The coos and awes shift me from Tevin's loving stare, and I realize I almost miss my baby girl coming down the aisle. I giggle and wave my fingers at her as she waves to me. She beams and sits tall in her wheelchair like the royalty she is as the pallbearer pushes her down the aisle. Nova begged Nina to let her still be flower girl, and honestly, Nina would've never told her no.

Tevin steps out of line once the two reach the front and tilts his head to the young boy to take his place while he takes his place and pushes Nova into the space slightly in front of me. Before he leaves, he leans in and kisses me on the cheek, and I know I am beet red and my face split with a huge girlish smile. I hear the girls behind me humming with amusement.

"Oh, my God, you two are sickeningly cute," Fallon whispers to me, just as the piano instrumental comes alive with a soothing alto voice layering on it, signaling Nina's ascend.

The gasps that roll over the guests are well-deserved. My girl looks beautiful, and I feel my eyes tearing up again as she makes her way down the aisle. Her dress is a beautiful Cinderella ballgown, fitting for the dreamy girl Nina is. At one point, Nina used to act like she didn't believe in the fairytale of love, but I knew her better than that. She loved love, and unfortunately, the wrong one took a bite out of her apple and turned her garden of love brown. That's until she lit that bitch, literally, and met her fireman Prince Charming. My girl is getting her fairytale, and I love that for her.

My thoughts continue to rave over how happy I am

for Nina as the ceremony begins, eventually trickling into the memories of how Fallon and Deacon found their love. Deacon pulled my girl out of her hoe phase and made her a housewife. Ha! I'm playing. She wasn't really a hoe, but my girl had her fun before Deacon changed the locks to her heart. Talk about risking their jobs and everything for love!

"You set my heart ablaze and make me feel alive over and over. You're my Fire Goddess until eternity…"

"Fasho…"

Tevin's out-of-line yet comical adlib to Denzel's vowels causes a low chuckle to peel through the groomsmen line, and Denzel cuts his eye at him before chuckling and continuing his vowels. When Tevin looks at me, I bulge my eyes at him and mouth "Behave." He shrugs and turns on his boyish grin.

My silent scold did nothing. When the nuptials were sealed and the reception began, Tevin turned the party up. Front and center on the dance floor—with me in tow!

The life of the party. That's always going to be my Tevin. That's what drew me to him the day I met him. He always had something funny coming out of his damn mouth. He matched my wit, and he was hella fine. Fun. Funny. And can fuck. It's a combination that turned us into the best of friends with benefits. Who would've thought I would fall in love with the one I wasn't supposed to? He was supposed to be just the young firefighter who turned the heat up in my bedroom, but when the smoke dissipated, there he was, reflecting feelings I didn't know could be ignited in me. Security. Acceptance. Love.

"Tevin, you will be responsible for carrying me out of this place," I hiss playfully yet very seriously to him. My feet were grateful for the slow tempo as one of the many Beyoncé songs Nina requested the DJ to play. "These shoes are not meant to be standing on all night!"

Tevin tightens his arms around my waist and offers, "Here. Put your feet on top of mine and I'll support you so you don't have to put weight on them."

My jaw drops at the suggestion, but I do it, lightly placing my feet on his spit-shined shoes. He lifts me just enough that I feel relief sweeping over my aching dawgs.

I giggle at how his silly suggestion actually works as he rocks us side to side. "Tevin, there's never a dull moment with you. You know that?"

He tilts his head, wearing that boyish grin from earlier again, and shrugs. "Never will be. Told you, you're my Gina to my Martin."

I drop my head back, sending my laugh into the air. "Tell me again, how does that work?"

He twists his mouth at me as if I were asking the silliest question of all time. "C'mon, Joni. You know. Gina was the *level-headed* one out of the couple..." He pauses and widens his eyes, letting his subliminal joke of

Gina's forehead settle until I catch on. I crack up. He continues after I come down, "Martin, he was a clown. He kept their relationship alive and young."

I scoff, pulling back, pouting my lips. "What are you trying to say, I'm old?"

Tevin groans and snatches me back to him. "Noooo. That's not what I'm saying, *Joni.*" He pecks my pouting lips, making me blush. "I'm just saying, we're the perfect balance. You bring me down to ground level when I need it, and I…I like to say I keep the spark in your eyes shining. Perfect balance."

I chew on my lip as the heat of the moment washes over my body. Goddamn, Tevin. There he goes, setting my body smokin' again. I inhale sharply and then exhale, cooling myself off. The lyrics of the Beyoncé song playing pique my ears when she hits the bridge. The lyrics hit me personally, too, as they seem to resonate deeply with me.

> *"What I'm gonna do is be a*
> *woman and let you be a*
> *man….*
> *I rather give up everything than to*
> *live my life with you…*
> *I would rather die young…than*
> *live my life without you."*

"That shits deep," Tevin whispers, obviously referring to the lyrics. His breath tickles my ear as we are now holding on to each other, body to body, and now in languid rock.

"Yeah," I crack, floating in the resonance of the lyrics. "I feel her, though."

A short laugh rumbles in Tevin's throat as he rubs circles in my back. "Hmph, is that right?"

I shift slightly just as he does, and our eyes meet, our lips graze. "Yeah. I can't imagine life without you as a part of it."

Tevin blinks slowly, and I catch a ghost of a smile in the corner of his mouth. In a whisper, he says the most affirming words before sealing it with the lock of our lips, "There will never be a life that we aren't together. Believe that."

And I do. With every morsel of my bones, I believe that life will never be lived without us being together. I love this for me.

ABOUT THE AUTHOR

Danielle Brooks hails from Richmond, Virginia, with a lifelong love for writing and reading. In 2023, Danielle Brooks embarked on her journey as a Contemporary Romance author. She is most notable for her Firefighter Romance series, Fire Company 143, but has released over 10 books with Black Love as the focal point. Currently, Danielle Brooks resides in Richmond with her two children, family and friends.

http://www.daniellebrookswrites.com
https://beacons.ai/daniellebrookswrites

ALSO BY DANIELLE BROOKS

Sweet Like Sundays

Kindred Moments

<u>Lennox Protective Services Series</u>

Flight to Parris

To Parris, With Love

Midnight: A New Year's Eve Novelette

<u>Belafonte & Friends Series</u>

Just Kickin' It (Prelude)

Kenderella

Friendsgiving With The Belafontes

Rings

<u>Fire Company 143 Series</u>

Smoke Signals

Through The Fire

Smoke & Mirrors

<u>In The Heart of Stonecrest</u>

Vanessa & Jericho, Season 1

www.ingramcontent.com/pod-product-compliance
Lightning Source LLC
Chambersburg PA
CBHW070621300726
48975CB00006B/1887